D0431348

First published in Great Britain in 2008 by Comma Press
3rd Floor, 24 Lever Street, Manchester M1 1DW
www.commapress.co.uk

A CIP catalogue record of this book is available from the British Library

ISBN 1-905583-22-2
EAN 978-1-905583-22-5

The publishers gratefully acknowledge assistance from the Arts Council England North West, as well as the support of Literature Northwest.

www.literaturenorthwest.co.uk

Set in Bembo by XL Publishing Services, Tiverton
Printed and bound in England by SRP Ltd, Exeter.

BRACE

A New Generation in Short Fiction

Edited by
Jim Hinks

CONTENTS

CONTENTS

Introduction

Short stories have a reputation for being demanding, and for good reason. Short stories demand our participation. They urge us to fill in the blanks, the spaces between the words.

Hemingway talks of the 'iceberg' effect – where eight-tenths of the story lurks below the waterline; Eudora Welty, of the short form's characteristic reticence: 'opaque by reason of intention.' Short stories, above other prose forms, insist that we reach into this latent realm of the unsaid, to fathom for ourselves a meaning that the novel would try to lay out before us.

There's a reason that short fiction, in particular, operates in this way. When reading a story, the effect of what we might call temporal de-emphasis (by which I mean that the last bit you read eclipses that which has gone before by simple virtue of being the most recent) is not so marked as when reading a novel. While the novelist is compelled to ink-in more and more detail as the novel progresses – to be ever more explicit in order to orientate the reader and prevent the whole enterprise from falling apart – the short story writer trusts that by the time we've finished reading a story, we can still remember the beginning pretty clearly. If we can absorb the text in one go, we can handle more subtext, as intellectual resources that would otherwise be devoted to retaining explicit information are freed to investigate the implicit. So it is that in short stories a good part of the action is implied – it happens off the page. They are, as Flannery O'Connor would have it, short in length but 'long in depth.'

I'd venture that this explicit/implicit ratio is what makes the best of short stories so compelling; it's how they get under your skin and stay there long after you've put the book down. Getting the balance right – deciding what to say and what to leave unsaid – is something their writers devote considerable attention to.

Richard Ford recently argued that the success of a short story is contingent on a writer's 'importance-making' decisions about what to show the reader. He quotes Henry James' preface to *Roderick Hudson*, which contends that, '…Really, universally, relations stop nowhere… the exquisite problem of the artist is eternally to draw, by a geometry of his own, the circle within which they shall happily appear to do so.' Ford (and James before him) were primarily referring to decisions about which characters, events, lines of dialogue and so on, to include on the page: the mise-en-scène of a fictional world. But it could also be said that the skilful short story writer draws, by a geometry of their own, a circle of *subtext*, signposting to the reader the perimeters of that which is at issue but which is *unsaid*. Hemingway's metaphor was well chosen: he knew that the tips of his icebergs insinuate their dimensions, their extent, below the waterline.

Take a look at a classic example of the form: Katherine Mansfield's 'The Fly'. We see the boss of a large firm, installed in a plush 1920s office, being visited by an old acquaintance. The visitor tells him that, when his daughters were recently in Belgium laying flowers on their brother's war grave, they also saw the grave of the boss's son. The visitor presently departs, and the boss sits in his office, thinking about his dead son and trying, without success, to cry. The second part of the story concerns itself with the boss rescuing a fly from the inkwell on his desk. He watches the fly slowly clean its wings, then inexplicably drops more ink onto it. The fly, again, cleans itself. The pattern repeats – three times, four times – before the fly runs out of fight, and dies.

It seems certain that the prominent elements of the story – the boss's status, the death of his son, and killing the fly –

have something to do with each other, otherwise they surely wouldn't *be* there. But what? What are we to make of his idle cruelty? Is he attempting to access feelings of grief that he couldn't otherwise experience? Is he trying to reassert some authority on a world over which, since the death of his son, he has little control? Has his bereavement left him devoid of sympathy?

Mansfield is unforthcoming. Yet while she refuses to connect the starkly rendered events of the story for us, they surely indicate its subterranean dimensions, as the extent of an oilfield is suggested by the position of derricks on the landscape. 'When I write, I reckon entirely upon the reader to add for himself the subjective elements that are lacking in the story,' said Chekhov. It seems that Mansfield was of the same mind, knowing that were she to bring the latent meaning to the surface, to tell the reader what to think, 'The Fly' would lose much of its potency.

The fifteen stories in this anthology are also peopled with troubled characters who do mysterious things, make seemingly inexplicable decisions that needle you long after you've finished reading. The reticence their writers employ is more than a reflex action – a formula absorbed in workshops, and deployed in their writing without discrimination – but is, in each case, a very specific opaqueness, put to very particular use. Take Guy Ware's 'Witness Protection', in which scenes of psychological breakdown and violence gradually begin to emerge from the whites of the page. The story points to issues of duality, upheaval, loss of self; piquing our interest with carefully deployed hints about the protagonist's uncertain past. But the author is careful to never entirely show his hand, knowing that it is this very ambiguity which generates tension.

There are lyrical stories here, too. Stories in which a pervading image chimes against the epical aspect (the plot events), and resonates long after the story has closed. These images are various, and carefully chosen. Jacqueline

McCarrick uses a trail of petals, Chris Killen a portrait, Paul de Havilland a carousel, Juliet Bates, the geometry of a landscape. Each image has its role to fulfil; indicating the subterrain of the story, pointing us towards an emotional dimension that the characters are unable to fully articulate.

Charlotte Allan's 'Memoirs of a Boy Genius' takes a different approach, as the inexplicably skewed world of the narrator plays delightfully against the 'real' world, *our* world, with all its familiar mores. It's when these two forces collide, as they inevitably must (the fictive version of the Amazon meeting the Atlantic), that a wave of transcendental meaning – something unvoiced, and far greater than the sum of the two parts – crests us to the end of the story.

Allan's is one of several stories here that locate their characters in strange, and ultimately impossible worlds. Perhaps liberated by a change in time or location or circumstance, these stories reject the conservative narrative voices which permeate realist short fiction, taking instead a more expansive, and sometimes satirical tone. This doesn't mean they give up their secrets easily; their mysterious confederations of the familiar and the far-fetched do not yield to reductive explanations. But if we are to go prospecting for subterranean meanings, we might begin by planting a spade at the point where the unreal/illogical/fantastic articulates something that its conventional or 'realistic' analogue could not.

Neil McQuillian and Heather Richardson follow yet another path, with stories that exemplify what Austin M Wright calls the 'recalcitrance' of the short form. Through the careful de-emphasis of characters, objects, or seemingly extraneous information (later revealed to be more significant than the reader first imagined), these stories purport to be one thing and then mutate into another. McQuillian's 'Old Man In A Tracky' sets out its stall as a sensuous, lyrical story, before in a coup de grâce a plotty, external dénouement falls into place. Richardson's 'The Doll Factory', beyond being a speculative story about moral jurisdiction and the military covenant, evolves into something else entirely, as the reader is always kept at a tantalising remove from the action. For these writers, a sudden change in tack or shift in emphasis doesn't disrupt the story, it *is* the story. It's the malleability of the form itself that allows them to keep the latent meaning held back, right until the end.

It's to be hoped that the stories in this anthology will entertain and engage the reader for as long as the pages are open. If their brevity and reticence leave you wanting more, all the better. If, days after you've finished reading, you find yourself wondering about them, trying to work them out (even trying to shake them off), better still. They're doing what they're supposed to. They're making demands of you.

Jim Hinks
January 2008

Witness Protection

GUY WARE

The house he wanted had a shallow porch. He found it at the end of a cul-de-sac, part of a new estate grafted onto the village. The houses were all built of faded yellow brick. They were not identical and did not face in the same direction. But, all the same, they pressed too hard against an acid green field of winter wheat: the edges were too square, the fences too sharp to pass. No one could suppose that these houses had not been built together in the same, new century. It was perfect for his purposes. Nobody here would have roots that had not been recently severed.

The outer door was open and he stepped inside, out of a light rain. A waxed cotton coat, still damp, hung from a peg above a pair of small, muddy boots. She could not have been back long herself. Odd, he thought: he would have expected her to be waiting. Surely they had told her it would be today? There were two glass panels in the inner door, but the glass was mottled and he could see nothing through it but dark shadows. There did not appear to be a bell. He knocked on the glass.

A woman opened the door. She was about his age, slightly younger, perhaps; slight – skinny, even – with a wide face and pale skin. Her dark hair was pulled back from her ears and high forehead; a few strands had worked free and

1

gathered in a loose, airy tangle at her temple. She was wearing jeans and a cap-sleeved shirt that showed her upper arms and seemed, in a woman of her age, defiant. The muscles of her arms were smooth. She looked strong, he thought, tempered. Not particularly attractive.

Ah, well, he thought. You tell yourself not to expect too much, but you can't help it. She was a woman, after all; it was a possibility. After what they'd said about her, he'd had his hopes.

She said, 'You're wet.'

'I told them not to bother bringing me right to the door. Only have to turn the ambulance round to get back out.'

There was a piano in the living room, with a row of framed photographs along the top. The piano itself was plain, unadorned – a functional box, not an item of furniture. On the rack, there was an open score: scrofulous gothic blots, slashing lines and elongated arrowheads scarred the creamy paper.

He said, 'Do you play?'

She handed him a mug of tea, made sure he had hold of it, before answering. 'You do, remember?'

'Of course.' Of course he did. He had only been there – been *home,* he should start saying – an hour. Already he was allowing himself to relax, to lose his grip on the brief.

He stood, put the mug down carefully, and walked over to the piano. He picked up the score. Schubert. He flipped through the pages. Christ, he thought. I can't do that.

Then: Of course I can't. Guy had been ill. *I've* been ill. That was their point.

In the hour since he'd arrived she – Stella, that is; it was time he brought himself to use her name – had asked if he would like a cup of tea, had shown him to the room he would be sleeping in, and had left him to wash and change. He had no clothes of his own, other than those he had on. Guy must

2

have used this spare room for dressing, however: the wardrobe was full. He chose a pair of cord trousers and a blue and white striped shirt. He found socks and old, well-polished brogues. He stepped back to look at himself, at Guy, in the mirror on the back of the wardrobe door. The clothes were good – old and soft – but all slightly too large. He had been ill, he told himself; he had lost weight. He put on an extra pair of socks; the shoes would be all right.

The shirt cuffs hung loose around his wrists: they would need links.

There was a leather case on a shelf in the wardrobe. In it, each nestled in its appropriate velvet depression, he found a pair of hairbrushes – leather backed with silver bands – two pairs of nail scissors of different size and a tortoiseshell comb. The bristles on the brushes were soft. There was a small compartment with a lid that he lifted to reveal an assortment of cufflinks, tie clips and a pair of elasticated metal bands that he thought might have been used to hold shirtsleeves in place. He slipped them on, and the slight constriction around his biceps made him feel as if he were donning armour. He chose a pair of cufflinks: small, flat gold ovals linked by thin chains. On one of each pair was engraved a crest he recognised. Guy had been an Old Wellingburian ('75–'80 Parker House): he had been there when there were still boarders; he was there, in the lower sixth, when the first girls arrived. The cufflinks were too small to reproduce the school's bracing motto, *Salus in Arduis,* which, in this mealy-mouthed age of personal growth, the school preferred to translate as 'Fulfilment through challenge'. All this he knew, or remembered, or had been told.

When he came downstairs, Stella had laughed. She said the armbands made him look like an Edwardian bank clerk, and he took them off. She said they were his father's: didn't he remember? So were the cufflinks.

Guy's father had been an Old Wellingburian ('28–'38 Platts), too, he recalled: at least he had died before his son.

She said, 'Would you like to play something now? It might help.'

'Wouldn't it disturb you?'

'Oh, you know me.' Her voice sounded fragile.

He nodded. 'Of course.' He wondered for a moment if he should wink, if she would appreciate it. No. This was a part he would have to get used to. Knowingness, irony, would have to go; it could get him killed. Her too, perhaps. Stella was doing him the courtesy of playing it straight; it was up to him to respond, to follow the rules.

'I won't, thank you. I'm a little tired.'

He replaced the score, and looked at the photographs: he – Guy, he should say – and Stella, dressed for a wedding, their wedding; Stella with a small boy and a baby; Guy holding the same baby; Guy with Jason and Annabelle, both in their prep school burgundy blazers; Jason outside the Parker-Steyne's House building in the blue uniform of the Senior School. (They had been two houses in Guy's day.) They'd done a good job with the photographs, he had to give them that. You couldn't see the joins.

Stella said, 'Of course. Have you eaten?'

They dined in intermittent silence and conversation no less uncomfortable than that of any blind date. They both wanted the evening to pass without difficulty. He praised the food, comparing it favourably to that in the hospital. She laughed and said she should hope so. Her laugh came out surprisingly deep, he thought, for someone of such slight build. She had changed into a blouse through which he could occasionally see the outlines of her bra – a bra which did not contain much to interest him. She was still wearing the jeans, which had traces of mud around the calves.

'The weather seems to have improved,' he said. 'It was pretty rotten this afternoon.'

'Yes.'

'Had you been out for a walk when I arrived?'

She didn't answer for a while. 'I went to visit the grave.'

'Ah.'

This was awkward, difficult, but he did not think he could change the topic without appearing callous. He had assumed they would have cremated her husband's body, made him disappear in smoke: a grave was always a potential loose end. Still, it wouldn't be the husband's name – his name now – on the stone, that much was certain.

'It would have been her birthday.'

She had meant Annabelle, the daughter. Thank Christ for that, he thought. Then: You've got to get a grip on the details.

'Of course,' he said.

She said there was just fruit for dessert; there might be some ice cream in the freezer. He said an apple would be fine.

After dinner he wanted to go straight to bed; he was tired. Coffee at this time of night would keep him awake, he said, then make his dreams worse.

He didn't say that he already knew – that he could tell her now if he chose to – exactly what he would dream about. The colours might vary. On some nights they would be heightened, saturated: the blood would look like pillarbox gloss as it pooled on the train floor. On others they were bleached, drained, and the blood would look more like brown sauce as it spread across the floor. Daddies Sauce.

So was it red or brown?

He'd have to say red. It was blood, after all.

They said he should only say things he knew to be true. Anything else would only cause trouble later.

Then they fed him lies.

This you know to be true, they said: your name is Guy West. You are forty-four. Your parents divorced when you were thirteen; you went to Wellingborough School, your father's alma mater. You married Stella West, nee Harris, in

1984. You had two children: Jason and Annabelle. Jason is nineteen and studying Anthropology at Bristol University; Annabelle died four years ago, at the age of twelve. You were a production manager, initially in the leather goods industry, and later – after the trade collapsed – in light engineering. (Out of the frying pan and into the fire, they allowed themselves to joke: you were not lucky in your choices.) You travelled regularly on business: to India, to Pakistan. When the engineering plant, too, closed recently, you were made redundant. You became depressed and ill. You were treated at St Andrew's Hospital in Northampton. You are now returning home, where you will require a lengthy period of convalescence.

All this you know to be true.

He did. He knew it.

'Good night,' he said. He hesitated, then stepped forward and kissed her lightly, on the cheek. He felt her watch him climb the stairs.

★

In the morning, she was brisk.

'How would you like your eggs?'

She had risen before him, showered and dressed. She was wearing jeans again, a clean pair. He was still in his pyjamas.

She made a pot of coffee.

'How are you feeling?' she said. 'Did you dream?'

'Just the usual.'

'What's the usual?'

He paused, put down his toast. 'I can't tell you – for your own protection.'

She laughed, and he said, 'I saw someone die.'

'Yes,' she said. 'That's not so unusual.'

6

But, she thought, she hadn't seen *him* die. She wasn't even sure when it had happened. Ten years ago, perhaps – when the travelling had started and they'd seen so little of him? Four years ago? Or three, when they'd moved here? When the factory closed? Or when he'd gone into that place? He was different now – there was no denying it – but why had she not spotted the change? Why had she not done something to prevent it?

Now she was left with this… impostor, and she blamed herself.

He said, 'He was listening to Mahler. That's why I noticed him.'

'Who?'

'The man who died. They didn't like that.'

'You don't kill someone for listening to Mahler.'

He meant, they hadn't believed him, he said.

'I know, Guy.'

She stood behind his chair, then leaned forward and wrapped her arms around him, rested her face on his shoulder. He did not move. He was thinner, harder. She could feel the parts that he was made of.

He had been ill, she thought. He was not yet better.

She persuaded him to walk into the village. She would have to drive into town later, to stock up properly now that he was back, but she needed to pay the paper bill and would buy a few things in the village shop. They were lucky to have it, she said. They should do their bit.

The older houses were low, plump piles of ochreous sandstone. The stone looked soft to Stella, as if she could scratch her name in it with a fingernail, only to see it washed away the next time it rained.

The shop sold newspapers and familiar tinned foods. The owner had recently installed a chilled cabinet and begun to display cheese and meat from local farmers, alongside mozzarella from Italy and sausages from Poland. She was behind the counter when they arrived, cutting chunks of organic Leicester from a wheel and wrapping them in cellophane.

'Morning, Stella. Lovely to see you again, Mr West. How are you?'

Guy said, 'Better, thank you.'

Stella offered a conspiratorial smile to the shopkeeper. 'He's still not quite himself.'

They left the shop and Stella led them through the churchyard, where the oldest tombstones had been elbowed into rows to make way for the more recently deceased. She climbed a stile and led them onto a muddy footpath beneath wet, bare trees. 'I thought we could go the long way home,' she said. 'Get a breath of air.'

She walked quickly, and had to pause from time to time to let him catch up. He had been ill, she told herself, but still. She wanted him to talk again, and she forced herself to slow down.

She had woken during the night and heard his voice. She'd stood at the door, listening to the rhythm of his speech, but could not make out the words. She thought he was most likely still asleep, and had returned to her bed – their bed – where she lay awake until dawn.

Crossing a ploughed field, helping him avoid the mud, she said, 'Which Mahler was it?'

'Five. The death march.'

She laughed again; she couldn't help it.

'You see?' he said. 'You wouldn't believe it either.'

Was he sure, they'd said, that this young man – this twenty-year-old plasterer from Poland, in his work clothes, innocent and with no idea what was about to happen – was it likely that he'd have been listening to Mahler's Fifth Symphony? Was it likely that the shots the five policemen fired into the back of his head would match the rhythm of the music?

It was possible.

It was possible, certainly. But was it likely? Was it *credible?*

He didn't know, he could be wrong, but that was what he remembered.

They said if he could not be sure, it was best not to mention it.

They said the man was large, his clothes were not clean. He would have sat with his legs splayed, his large work boots planted firmly out in front of the adjoining seats: surely he would have noticed that?

It was almost raining again now. A soft dampness resolved from a silver-grey sky, diffracting the light into an opaque, directionless miasma. The fields looked somehow larger than usual, flatter, deprived of any shadows. Sheep grazed listlessly. She pointed out to Guy, as she had before, the regular corrugations, the thousand year-old marks left in the landscape by the strip farming of medieval peasants. She turned into the access road that led into the estate, felt the slight incline in the muscles of her legs. There were no real hills in this part of the country, but the road – the estate itself – cut across the contours of the land it occupied.

'Are you all right?' she said, when they were back indoors, their coats and boots left drying in the porch. 'That wasn't too much for you?'

'I'm fine. But I think I'll stay here this afternoon.'

*

The telephone rang while Stella was out. He considered letting it ring, but thought he'd better get used to this some time. He found the phone and picked it up. It was light and cordless, like a mobile. He pressed the green button.

'Guy West.' He almost swallowed the name.

'Dad?'

It was Jason. His mind churned; he said nothing. Into the silence, Jason said, 'Hi. You're back.'

'Yes.'

'How are you feeling now?'

'I'm better than I was.'

There was a pause.

'That's good. Is Mum there?'

'No. No, she's in town, I'm afraid. Shopping.'

'Well, I hope she's getting plenty in. Turns out I can come tomorrow after all. Tell her I'll stay over, will you? There's nothing here I can't miss on Monday.'

'All right.'

'And tell her I'm sorry I couldn't make it for Bella's birthday, yeah? But I'll see her tomorrow, yeah?'

'Yes.'

'And you Dad. Good to have you back.'

★

Stella said, 'You'll have to sleep with me tomorrow.'

'Why?'

'Because we've only got two bedrooms here. Because otherwise Jason will think there's something wrong. You know what the young are like.'

Over dinner that night, he told her everything. He was not Guy West. He was not her husband. (She would know this already, of course.) He'd never been to Wellingborough; he was not a redundant production manager. He was a witness. His name was Henry Fielding, and he had seen a man killed − executed − by five armed policemen on a Midland Mainline train. The man was unarmed. He was innocent − there had been some terrible mistake − but that was not the policemen's story.

She said, 'It's all right, Guy. I know.'

'I'm not Guy, I'm Henry. I'm a witness. I saw it.'

But what had he seen? In his sleep now, he told her, he sees the man's splayed thighs. His jeans are dirty. The right thigh, the one nearest to him, moves up and down to the rhythm of some unknown, unheard music; his foot taps soundlessly, despite the heavy boot. Already, he said, he knows that what he sees is not what he saw.

In the night she heard his voice again.

She stood at the door, listening. She was wearing a long tee shirt; her legs and feet grew cold. She opened the door. It was dark, darker than her room, but she could make out his body, curled away from her. The duvet had slid, or been kicked, onto the floor. She picked it up, lay quickly on the bed and pulled it over both of them.

He did not move; his mumbling continued.

She rolled onto her side, pressed herself against him, fitting her knees into his, her breasts against his back, her left arm around his chest. She wondered where to put her other arm: in this position there was never anywhere for it to go.

Gradually his murmuring subsided, then stopped. She managed to get comfortable, and they slept.

In the morning she woke before he did. He had rolled onto his front, his face pressed sideways into the pillow, one arm raised, the other trailing out behind him. He looked like the chalk outline of a murder victim one might see in a film or on the cover of a crime novel.

She smiled. Even asleep he was pretending, dramatising.

But was there anything so terrible about that? If he wanted to be someone else, to pretend his real life was just a cover story, so what? What harm would it do? Reality had not done him any favours, she thought. Or her.

She rolled him onto his back. He felt surprisingly light. She examined his body as if she had never seen it before. She traced her finger along his sternum, felt ribs where before there had been soft, doughy flesh. The stomach was flatter, the hip bones more pronounced. The familiar bifurcated form of a man looked strange and new. As she continued her inspection, his penis stirred, grew, twitched and stood upright.

She checked that he was still asleep, then stroked it gently, rubbing it with the smooth skin on the inside of her wrist. She knelt, leaned over and licked it tentatively, took it into her mouth, something she had never done before. As he woke, she threw her leg across his thighs and sat up. She leaned forward until her face was close to his, his penis pressed against her belly.

'Henry,' she whispered. 'Wake up.'

She kissed him on the mouth.

'How would you like your eggs, Henry?'

★

When Jason arrived, Henry – watching from the dining room through a crack where they'd left the door ajar – thought at first that he looked a little like the Polish plasterer. This happened a lot, Henry knew. Jason was fair, not dark, his hair long and almost curly, his chin half-covered by a ragged beard, where the Pole had been clean-shaven; but they had the same loose-limbed physical confidence. The same way of more than filling the space they occupied. Watching him, Henry thought it obvious that he could not have spawned this blonde monster. Jason was nearly a foot taller than his mother, but she was strong and they embraced in the hallway vigorously, as equals. When they released each other, Jason turned towards the dining room, towards Henry, arms outstretched.

Instinctively, Henry stepped backwards, but Jason was only shrugging the small backpack from his shoulders.

Stella said, 'Jason, I'm sorry. Didn't you get my message?'

'Sorry, Mum, my mobile's died. What was it? Did you want me to pick something up on the way here?'

She said, 'You can't stay. In fact, you can't come in.'

She told him she was sorry, that his dad had thought he'd be OK but that, now it came to it, he wasn't. That he wasn't up to seeing anyone yet, not even Jason.

'But Mum...'

She told him not to worry, she'd be all right. She told him to stay locally, in town – she gave him some cash. She'd call him later.

'My mobile's dead, remember?'

Then she'd meet him, tomorrow. Lunchtime tomorrow. But now he had to go.

She pushed him out, still protesting, and locked the door behind him. She turned, leaning against the door as Henry emerged from the dining room. She laughed, wild and raw, a sound that shocked them both for a moment. Then they collided, Stella tearing at his clothes, struggling to shrug off her jeans, Henry holding her face in both hands, kissing her mouth desperately.

'Upstairs,' she said, but they didn't make it.

'Henry,' she said, later. 'When's the trial?'

He was half-asleep. The sun, low in the early afternoon, sliced through the blinds, lighting corrugated strips on the duvet. Her head was on his shoulder, her hair spread across his chest.

He said, 'Trial?'

'You know, the trial.'

'Oh. Sometime in the Spring, maybe. They weren't sure.'

She pressed herself closer, her leg hooked across his waist, her groin sticky against his thigh.

'And you'll still need protection, won't you? When it's over?'

'They didn't say.'

'But they couldn't just abandon you?'

He said nothing for a while. 'I suppose not.'

★

13

In the morning she was sluggish. She had to be in town, at work, by nine or thereabouts, but she found it hard to get going. She would be seeing Jason at lunchtime.

After Jason left – let's be honest, she thought: after she had thrown him out – they had spent the whole day in bed, emerging only to scavenge for food and drink, padding naked around the house and hurrying back to the asylum of the bed, the comfort of warm flesh. When, if ever, had she last done that? Probably when she was a student, when she'd met Guy. Certainly not since Jason was born.

It was raining again. The traffic was bad and she was late for work, but nobody noticed; it was not that kind of job. She was lucky, she supposed.

She and Guy had done all right for sex, she thought. That had not been the problem. Even after the children, even when he got his new job, they'd always found the time, the energy; whenever he wasn't away. And, after Annabelle died, they'd made love more, not less – at least for a while – grasping at each other with an intensity, a viciousness, she thought now, that betrayed them. Then it had tailed off, as things do.

In the end he'd moved into the spare room. It made sense: he wasn't well and she wasn't sleeping. Then, of course, he'd moved to St Andrew's and the question hadn't arisen.

Yesterday, late in the evening, she'd said, 'Henry, you're married, aren't you?'

He looked at her. 'Oh yes.'

'Then I suppose this can't last.'

He didn't reply.

'Do you have children?'

'Yes,' he said, not realising the stakes. 'A boy and a girl.'

Her body had stiffened against his; neither of them said anything more.

At noon she was interrupted in a meeting: reception had a Jason West to see her. It was early for lunch, and she had

14

arrived late, but there was nothing for it, she would have to make her excuses and go.

That morning, before she'd left for work, he'd told her about the Mahler again. He *had* heard Mahler. It might not be credible, but it was true. Hurrying to get out of the house, she had said, 'I know, Guy. You've told me before.'

Now she wondered what she would say to Jason, how she could explain herself. She had made such a big thing about him coming home that weekend, even though it was his first term at university. He would be angry with her, she thought, and rightly so.

She saw him standing in reception, the image of his father. A slightly enlarged image, perhaps, but there was no mistaking the likeness. They hugged, Jason not letting go of her arms afterwards, as she pulled away.

'Mum, are you OK?'

'I'm fine.'

'What about Dad?'

She hesitated. 'He's... better. He's back to normal, Jason.'

'Is that good?'

She wouldn't answer that.

'I'm sorry about yesterday,' she said. 'It was all a silly mistake.'

It wouldn't happen again, she said, then asked him where he fancied going for lunch.

★

In the house on the edge of the estate, he wondered who Guy West was, anyway? When they cast around for an identity to hide him in, how had they alighted upon this public schoolboy failure – with the dead daughter and the giant of a son and the sexy, tiring wife? He couldn't have been completely clean. He must have been *known*; they had to have been aware that he was ill, that he might die, that

Stella would co-operate. He assumed the answer lay somewhere in India, or – more likely – Pakistan. It was not the most stable part of the world these days.

But it didn't really matter who Guy was, he thought. I might as well be him: at least until it's time to take the stand.

Old Man in a Tracky

Neil McQuillian

There were two things in the room that never looked right to him. There was the mobile phone by the radiator, always on, always plugged in, hot as a roast potato and never a peep out of it, and the white plastic bag with the tracksuit inside.

It had been there for months, since he got back from Thailand. He'd bought it for his son John. They were cheap out there of course but it was a proper one. Named. It said Lacoste on the inside and had a little crocodile emblem on the jacket and the kecks. Looked just like the ones all the young fellas wear. He'd thought it would be a good thing to buy, as a gesture, get them talking again. But when he'd come back and gone to John's place in Crosby with it, this girl he'd obviously been living with, skinny thing, she told him that John had cleared out, moved to Canada. The train back that day – all the families on their way home from Southport fair, and him sat staring out at the river, gripping tightly to that bag in his lap – bloody horrible.

And there it was, still in its bag, just sitting on the mantelpiece. It made the place look untidy. He emptied it out on to the bed, then unzipped the top and felt the lining – soft and thin, slightly see-through. It reminded him of sausage skin. He touched it to his groin, then put it on. Were you supposed to wear undies with these things? It was on now either way. He opened the wardrobe and his reflection swung giddily towards him in the mirror on the inside of the door. He stood like a boxer and stared at himself. The other day, on the train, there'd been some lads sitting opposite him who looked like just the sort of little hardnoses he used to enjoy coming up against when he was younger, and so he was watching them, waiting to catch their eye, wanting to know that people still felt it when he looked at them. But they'd just looked back, and then when they'd got off the train they'd banged on the window and pointed and laughed. He went up close to the mirror. He wanted to see again what they hadn't seen. That time with Kathy's dad and her uncle? Had their tails down after that. He headed out, rustling as he went down the stairs, the mobile phone in his pocket bumping his thigh.

Outside it was quiet and mild. It had rained overnight and he could smell red brick. He stood in the path and inspected himself in the daylight. Apart from the tiny green crocodiles, the tracksuit was pure, unbroken baby-blue. His brown slip-ons were a disgrace in comparison. They wanted replacing, or a good polish. He looked up and down the road, picking at the elasticated sleeves as if they were too tight. It didn't look like there was anybody about. He did the zip right up so that the collar sat erect over his chin, and went out the gate.

The tracksuit played up a little bit. As soon as he started walking the jacket ballooned out at the front, so he tucked it into the kecks. Then he had to sort out a drawstring that was tickling his groin. But once it was tamed it felt neat and tidy, smart in a way, and he could understand why all the lads wore them. It felt like it floated warmly around him, as if he was standing in one of those draughts they have above the doors in the big shops in town. It was a clever bit of design. It made you feel like running.

He strolled along, feeling calm. His arms swung gently, his testicles too, not impeded by underwear. It was almost a swagger. He remembered the time he went to New Brighton with the lads and they'd gone skinny dipping after an afternoon on the ale. He'd been the first to strip off and had walked across the car park, marched across it, starkers, with a smile that was too big for his face, imagining the lads all creased up watching from the car. He felt his nakedness under the tracksuit, and smiled that smile again.

As he went down the road he looked into the front room of each house, ready to wave. He stopped by one and shielded his eyes, peering into the relative gloom. A nice girl lived there with her little lad. But there was no television glow, and the sofa and armchair were empty. After he'd been round to John's that day, and the girl had said what she'd said and closed the door, he'd stood looking at the house for a while, then wandered round and round all the unfamiliar streets for a couple of hours. He remembered thinking how they've got all these great big houses out that way but not a bit of life coming from any of them. Not the way it used to be round here. Mustn't have been John's sort of place either.

He picked up the *Daily Post* and headed for Maurice's. The blossom was coming out everywhere. It was like being surrounded by pregnant women. As he walked along it smelled of walking to school or to the betting shop or to the vet's with Bridey.

Maurice shouted 'Hello' from somewhere in the back when he walked in and the bell jangled.

'Hello. It's Joey.'

'Be with yer in a second, Joe.'

It was dark inside. He sat down on the maroon banquette. The barber's chair obscured his view of the mirror so he slid across and stared through the dusty air at his reflection in the flaking, burnt-looking surface. His white face looked silvery grey in the gloom, like a sardine on a mudflat. He thought of his old cross-country trophies on the sideboard at home and took the mobile out of his pocket. He switched it off and then back on again, and watched the sequence it went through before it reached a state it seemed content with.

Maurice came down the small wooden flight of steps leading into the back of the shop, wiping his hands on his slacks.

'Just having a slash, Joe.'

Joe saw him glance at the tracksuit as he went to the door, to turn the sign round so 'Open' was facing inwards. He unzipped his jacket and sat down in the chair.

'Right then, here we go,' said Maurice. 'You're the first I've had in this week. Bloody ridiculous. Hang on a sec, just need to turn the telly off in the back.'

Three quid for three days work, thought Joe. How do these blokes do it? He must have a bit put away.

While Maurice saw to the telly, Joe looked at his reflection. His hair was still thick, still had a healthy look about it. It clung to him like lichen and he was proud of it. When John was still living round here, before he moved out to the posh parts, and he'd see him at the shopping precinct or going off somewhere on his bike, his hair was always cut down to the bone, like most of the young fellas round here, like his own when he was in the Merchant Navy, before he worked on the docks. Maurice reappeared.

'I suppose it's all skinheads these days Maurice.'

'And they can do it themselves can't they Joe? Or the missus does it, quick once over with the clippers, does the kids as well, and there you have it.'

Joe's forehead was wet from the spray Maurice used to dampen his hair, but he didn't try to wipe it away. The top half of his body was covered in a cloak, tightly secured round his neck.

'Suppose it saves them a few bob over a year,' he said. Regret immediately crystallized on both of them.

'I'll bet it bloody well does,' said Maurice. He stood square behind Joe and looked at him in the mirror. 'How's that for yer? What about those sidies?'

'Just leave half an inch or so.' Joe turned his head left and right. 'You know what, sorry Maurice, do you reckon you could take a bit more off?'

'Where, Joe? On top?'

He ran his fingers through his short back and sides, remembering what a buzz cut felt like.

'Do you reckon you can take it much closer with the scissors?'

'Yeah, there's a bit more to play with.'

'Let's go for it then. Short as you can.'

'Right you are, Joe. Look, I've got a set of clippers if that's what you're after?'

'Oh ey, Maurice. I'm sixty-six, don't be soft.'

'Thought you might have been looking to tail off, Joe.'

'My courting days are behind me, lad. Thank God.'

Maurice's oily scissors continued their squeak squeak birdsong.

'Still got the mobile, Joe?'

'Still got it.' He was going to say it was neither use nor ornament but it was Maurice who had given it to him.

'Bloody nuisance they are, you know,' Maurice continued. 'The grandkids are always sending me these text messages.'

Maurice's plump knuckles took tighter and tighter grips of Joe's hair, pulling at the scalp now. He watched his appearance change in the mirror.

'You're ringing there, Joe.'

Maurice put his scissors in the jar as this dawned on Joe. He started clambering out of the chair, startled, all jowls, trying to get the little chunk of plastic out of his thigh pocket. The mobile continued its hyperactive chorus as Joe held it in his hand, his forefinger hovering over the buttons. He focused on the screen. It said 'John'. John was calling him, and he couldn't answer the bloody scuthering thing.

'Help us out here, will you, Maurice.' His heart danced with the awful nervy ringing which he dreaded would finish before he could speak to his son. Maurice took it, mastered it,

21

then handed it back. Joe brought it to his ear, shaking a little now.

'John? That you son?' There was a pause. He heard traffic.

'Oh hello. No, no.' It was a woman's voice. Well-spoken. 'I'm just at a bus stop, and a man just got on a bus and left his phone here on the bench. I'm not sure what to do. I looked at his numbers and saw 'Dad'. I'm in Crosby. Are you anywhere nearby?'

Something huge swam into his head, dizzying him.

'A tall lad. Curly hair.'

'That's right, yes. With a blonde girl.'

The phone felt unnaturally hot against his ear. He thought of getting that Southport train to Crosby again.

'I'm not far away, love. Is there a shop there you can leave it with, tell them I'll come along in a bit?'

'Yes, I am on Endbutt Lane and there's a newsagent called Mapley's on the corner. I know them in there. I shall leave it with them. OK?'

'Right, I'll come and get it this afternoon. Endbutt Lane?'

'That's it. Well, goodbye.'

'Bye love, thanks.'

He passed the phone to Maurice and sat back down in the chair. Watching his slow steady progress he felt like grabbing the scissors and crunching, shredding at his hair with them. Their talk dried up.

When he got home he put the tracksuit back into the bag and put it in the wardrobe with Kathy's old dresses, then got changed into his own clothes. He stood in the big bay window and looked into the block of sky hanging over the docks, listening to the distant clanging and crashing of containers being unloaded, then looked northwards, towards Crosby. He put his cream Harrington jacket on, and went back down the stairs and out into the streets again, heading for the train station.

Lindy

ANNIE CLARKSON

We find Lindy in the park. A fat awkward girl, sweating in the heat with her jeans rolled up, trainers kicked onto the grass next to her. She sits in the dappled shade of a tree. Cross-legged. Picks at a scab on her hand. Reads from a paperback. We can't see the title. Her eyes dart up from the page sometimes, as if she might be looking for someone.

We sit near her, but she doesn't look in our direction, not once. We watch her tuck a strand of grease-slicked hair behind her ears. She's one of those grubby girls. Needs to wash more. Chews her nails. Wears too much black to hide her weight. She picks at the grass next to her bare feet and squints across the park, as though she's still waiting.

Twenty minutes pass and nobody comes. She makes no effort to move from the grass. Her book lies in her lap, the breeze flapping the pages open. We think she looks small here. A girl on her own in a vast field where students are drinking, couples share picnics, men play football.

We boil a kettle on the calor-gas stove we brought here. We unpack a jar of instant coffee, sachets of sugar, a carton of milk. It's all laid out on the grass in front of us and we argue quietly over who should be first to meet her. Martin thinks it should be me, he says I'm ready for it now. But the others want to draw straws, so Martin finds two long blades of grass and a

23

short one. He lines them up in his hand and holds them out.

I feel nervous, put my fingers out for the middle one. Make sure you're certain, he says, and his dark eyes narrow. I change my mind, shut my eyes, pull it out. Decided, Martin says.

I take a deep breath as I walk over. I put a friendly smile on my face, count backwards from ten. Excuse me, I say. She looks up, startled. Do you want a coffee? I ask, pointing back towards Martin and the others. We've got plenty. We thought you might want one.

She blinks at me. I can see she's searching for an answer. Her eyes doubtful. Teeth biting her bottom lip as if she's chewing the decision over. She looks young, younger than we thought. She might be sixteen, no more. I tell her, We're just being friendly, it doesn't matter if you don't want to.

I turn maybe forty-five degrees away from her, as if I might start walking back. But she says, No, don't go. I'm not sure. How many of you are there?

Four, I tell her. Martin. Me. Jonas. He's Danish. He's going back soon. And Fiona.

I notice all the badges on her bag. All the bands she must like. I say, you'll get on with Fiona. She likes all kinds of music – rock, thrash, metal.

I'm Lindy, she says holding out her hand. I wipe my damp hand on the back of my jeans and shake hers.

We learn that Lindy is away from home, lonely, homesick. She comes from a village in South Wales. None of us can pronounce the name properly. She has five brothers who are all older than her. They never let her do anything she wants. Always taking her places, picking her up, insisting on staying with her sometimes. At home, it was claustrophobic. But now I'm here, she says, it's like I miss them. Their noise in the mornings. Fighting over the bathroom. At least somebody cared where I was, she says.

Martin sits close to her. He puts his hand on her knee.

It's a subtle move, but deliberate. We all notice it. But Lindy doesn't. She carries on talking and Martin lets her, and we watch as she opens up more and more and the coffee gets cold and people start leaving the park as it's getting later in the day and cooler.

You should come back for tea, Martin says. She looks around the park, noticing other people have left. She stands up and brushes soil from her jeans. She fiddles with the badges on her bag, as though she's tidying them, but we know she's nervous. She's realising she doesn't know us. It's only been a few hours. She's aware she's been talking about herself, hasn't even asked about us.

We only live local, Martin says, and this makes her more nervous. She's clumsy with her trainers, trying to pull them on her heel at the same time as standing. Her weight makes this difficult. She almost loses her balance. Starts again. Leans against a tree while she tries to hurry, putting on first one trainer, then the other, without unfastening the laces.

Or we could go for a curry, he says, there's a great place over there, look. He points to Wilmslow Road. I've never had curry, she says. Never had curry? Martin repeats, and we all repeat it, saying how she must come for a curry, it would be a shame to miss out, all those nan breads and popadoms, and bhajis she's never tasted.

She wavers.

Before she can give an answer, the stove is packed up, the coffee, the stack of plastic cups. We're standing and walking with Lindy to the edges of the park. We're telling her how great it'll be, how lucky we feel to have found her, how it's obviously meant to be.

Lindy loosens up with alcohol. We order her a glass of wine, which she doesn't like, but drinks anyway. We order her a pint of Kingfisher and she drinks it too quickly so we order her another one. We laugh, say it must be the heat, how her body's probably dehydrated. We break up popadoms and dip them in raita and mango chutney and lime pickle. Martin puts a chunk of lime pickle on a bit of popadom and feeds it to Lindy. We watch Lindy's face flush with the heat from the pickle. She gulps from her third pint. Laughs.

She pushes her chair back from the table and staggers a little as if she didn't realise how much she'd drunk. Toilet, she says, her napkin dropping to the floor. Martin looks at me, his eyes following her as she walks across the restaurant, telling me to go after her.

I follow her to the bathroom. She's in the cubicle. I hear the zip of her jeans, the struggle of denim over wide hips, then a lengthy pause before her piss streams into the toilet bowl. It's endless. A pause, then a dribble. Lindy sighs while she pulls up her trousers. I switch the tap on and watch her in the mirror as she comes out. Hi Lindy, I say. She says, Oh hi. Washes her hands. Dries them on a paper towel. Your friends are so nice, she says. I smile at her reflection and agree.

Lindy tells us she lives in halls of residence. She's eighteen. Just. Her birthday is the end of August. She came here in September. She wanted to get away from home as soon as she could. She studies French and Psychology, joint honours. She's never been to France, but she had a French girl stay at their house once. It was an exchange organised by school. Only she didn't go and stay with the French family because her brothers didn't want her to go abroad alone.

She takes huge mouthfuls of chicken dhansak, stuffs herself with peshwari nan and tells us how she finds it hard to make friends usually. How she struggles to talk to people sometimes. We laugh and say, that doesn't seem like you Lindy, does it? No, that doesn't seem like Lindy. A giddy smile opens up her mouth while she's eating. We can see half-chewed bread clagging up her teeth. She has a smudge of grease on her chin. Martin wipes it off with his thumb. He says, you look pretty when you're smiling Lindy. Lets his fingers brush against her cheek, just for a second.

He reaches down under the table for his bag, rummages for his digital camera. He says, take a picture of me and Lindy. She shakes her head and says, no, don't, but we can see how pleased she is. She lets him put his arm around her so we can take a picture. We abandon our food and arrange ourselves around Lindy, ask a waiter to take our photo.

She squints at the pictures on the viewer. I look so awful, she says. Martin says, how can you say that Lindy? You're so pretty, and we all agree with him, tell her, you *are* pretty Lindy, can't you see it? We talk about her Marmite brown eyes, the way her nose turns up at the end, just a little, and how when she smiles, her whole face smiles. We say, has nobody ever said that to you Lindy? She shakes her head and her fringe falls across her face. Martin says, look, you're doing it now Lindy. Her face is a beetroot-blush, and he holds her hand under the table. She doesn't pull it away. In fact, she clings to him, flushed with beer and curry and the heat that still lingers in the air.

We invite Lindy back to our house. Just for a nightcap. A hot chocolate or a vodka, if she wants it. She kicks back two small shots of vodka and sinks into the cushions, talking with Fiona about Marilyn Manson and Korn and Queens of the Stone Age. They talk about a music festival that Lindy's never been to, and Martin says, maybe we can get tickets if you want, we could all go together.

Lindy is too pleased to speak. Eyes beer-glazed. A sweat-slick across her forehead. She throws her arms around his neck and he tickles her, won't let her go, makes her dance with him. We watch them, swaying in the middle of the lounge with no music. I hear myself telling Fiona, how happy I was when I first came here. Jonas is saying how gutted he'll be to leave. But we're all watching Lindy. She leans against his shoulder with her eyes closed. His arms round her waist, holding her, in the same way he held me. I remember feeling weightless. As if he might carry me. Lindy's feeling this too. I know it. I see Fiona glancing at her reflection in the mirror and she knows it too.

But, Lindy is lost in a music only she can hear. She laughs. A girl's laugh, playful, relaxed, flirtatious. She lets herself fall back onto the settee, carelessly. Her eyes are still closed, and she lets him touch her. Her neck. Her shoulder. The length of her arm. His fingers trail across her skin making lazy patterns.

He looks over at us. We keep talking, but the look is noted. It says, we're nearly there now. It won't be long. He lets his hand run down the outside of her thigh and she seems peaceful, almost asleep as he strokes her. He's telling her something. Quietly. I can't hear what he's saying, but I can imagine. He's telling her she shouldn't cover herself in so many clothes, she's got a gorgeous figure, and men love women with curves. He squeezes one of her thighs and slides his hand between them. He kisses her neck. He's still talking to her and she's laughing again, a giggly half-cut laugh. He unfastens her shirt without her even noticing. He does it button by button while he's distracting her with compliments.

When his hand strokes the bare skin of her stomach, she blinks her eyes wide open. He's close to her, almost on top of her. I hear him say, nobody's watching Lindy. His mouth quietens her.

But we all watch. Fiona has the camera. Martin gave it to her earlier. She holds it tight and I notice there are sweat pearls along the curve of her hand. I can feel her shaking. Jealousy maybe. Discomfort. How I felt when we first found Fiona.

Only Lindy isn't like me or Fiona. She tries to pull back. Struggles a little. I hear her voice, a small sound, almost involuntary. A moan, I think at first. But then I hear it as a quiet *no*. A tongue-bitten, almost swallowed *no*.

Martin is pressing his mouth against hers. He struggles

28

with the zip on her jeans, fights with it as she wriggles underneath him. She tries to lift her head. But he presses his hand flat against her forehead and pushes it down. He laughs. It's not a friendly laugh. We all stop talking, and look at Martin with unexpected questions. And at Lindy pinned down under Martin. He kneels on her legs, finally ripping open the zip on her jeans and she's making a strangled noise, almost suffocated. FOR FUCK'S SAKE LINDY, YOU'RE MAKING THIS DIFFICULT, he shouts, his body pressing down on her. He grabs a cushion, forces it over her face.

And I think, it isn't supposed to be like this. I hear my voice break into the room. Martin?

Can't you see I'm busy, he says, FUCK IS EVERYONE STUPID? You need to help me off with her pants. FAT BITCH. Fuck, these jeans are too tight.

She grabs at his clothes, his hair, pushing him away. Hold her arms, Martin says to nobody in particular and Jonas moves behind them, gripping hold of her, stopping her from moving. I stare at them, a jumble of arms and legs all struggling.

Was I like this? Fiona asks. She says my name and I find it hard to answer her. I clear my throat and say, not the same, no. She asks, I didn't struggle? No, I say. She's digging her nails in her palm. I can't stay in here, she says in a quiet voice. Almost silent.

We sit in the kitchen and wait for the kettle to boil. We try to block out the Lindy-noise by playing the radio loud. We sing, making up the words, shouting them over the radio, over the kettle boiling, over the other noise. We tap against the table with spoons, bang empty cups.

But we can still hear the crying. It's loud, louder than if we were Lindy, louder than anything. It's an inside noise. A noise that starts in our gut, and is forced into our chest. It bruises our throat. And grows until we can't hold it in any more.

Memoirs of a Boy Genius:
Organ Divine

Charlotte Allan

It was on the afternoon of my fourth birthday that I first met the great organ that exposed my genius. That is to say it was the day we called my birthday as of course, being a foundling, there was no way of being certain. As it happened, plans had been made for the previous day but the sky being grey and doomy we had postponed the celebrations; flexibility one has when there is no way of being certain. The sun shone on my birthday therefore, bright and illuminating as the spring day my parents found me wriggling on the motorway. Stood at the foot of the garden worrying about some broom my mother spied a bundle in the second lane, my father saw it move. Thinking it kittens they made the short journey down the embankment together, helping each other across the fence and the man-made scree before making a dash for me during a gap in the traffic. My parents were old to begin with and could easily have persuaded each other out of such a risk, but to my continuing benefit they didn't, and I was brought to safety. Unharmed by a hundred cars I puckered and frowned as they carried me back to the cottage and when they unwrapped me I had the expected number of teeny-tiny fingers and wee-little toes.

Had I been reported to the proper authorities at the time I would surely have been given an official and unwavering date of birth (accurate or not) but my parents feared and hated the Authorities as other people's parents feared and hated the Devil or the Bank or What People Must Think. They waited for reports of a missing baby and when, after a time, nothing was heard, they gave me a name and made me a bed. My own memories begin at a time where my mother folds herself down to my cot, scoops me up and carries me to the window to wave at my father, grubbing in the garden. The window to the garden is old and not yet adjusted to her towering height and my mother must kneel to see through it. Parts of the cottage have no ceiling below roof height in order that she may move about freely and when she sleeps it is on two divans pushed end to end. My father sees me waving and comes up to the window putting his palms against the glass. These palms, along with his nose, two shiny cheeks and a pair of twinkly eyes were the only parts of him I ever saw, the rest being covered in clothing, hair or both. Each new day is unusual to a toddler and I accepted my parents' oddities with the good grace of innocence. It was only much later, when my adventures began in a world beyond Mother and Father, that I made a connection between their isolated life in a cottage accessible only by dirt track or hard shoulder and their respective height and hairiness, excessive as they both were.

On the morning celebrated as my fourth birthday I was ignorant and happy. Untouched by the traditions of the outside world. I was given cake for breakfast. This may sound delightful but stale toast would have been kinder, or porridge with salt. Although an excellent cheese presser, master jam-boiler and all round good egg my mother was exceptionally bad at baking cakes. It was the size and shape of a cowpat with the taste and texture of the foamy olive blocks that florists make use of in tricky arrangements. Four candles pointed the directions of the compass and dripped wax onto the greening icing. I blew them out in one breath and wished for a better cake. Smiling in their beneficence the Gods looked into my soul and sent me a bicycle. 'Just to the bench now,' my parents said, and away I sped up to that single-slatted, nettle-backed neglected ex-bench that marked the brow of the hill and the edge of our world. I had not yet questioned the reason for this or any other boundary. Had I been forewarned that in less than a minute something amazing would happen that would change my life forever, I would not have understood: I had a bicycle.

I have three memories of greater importance than any of the others. I keep them in a separate and safer place and go to them when I am weary of all things else. They each lasted less than four seconds, time I have since multiplied into hours of pleasure as I labour to conjure the feelings again, as precise and as detailed as when first felt. The most recent, though it happened some thirty years ago, occurred after my first public performance of *The Mangrove Symphony* in Vienna. There was much gossip surrounding the event, unschooled oddity that I was, and I was convinced the hall was stacked full of eager critics and sour traditionalists. The last note had hummed from the belly of the cello and I stood, fingers white on baton, trapped in the viscous silence like a Neanderthal in ice. When I did turn, and the silence tipped into that blinding cacophony, that awful thunderous mess of sound that all musicians want to write, I felt the feeling I had only felt twice before. Previously I had been fifteen and alone in the darker parts of Helsinki. Tuami was gone, or rather she was gone from me, and my quest had closed without the great answer I had been hoping to find. I was without friends or purpose, the only two things one needs to survive, and I spent a long time walking and staring and knowing nothing. I was stood at the edge of a dock, singing my melancholy aria to the air when a lady called from a doorway, 'That, that is how I feel'. I turned and wanted to ask her how she knew to address me in English and how she had become so sad but she said only, 'Please, please don't stop', so I didn't. It was then that I knew for certain what had to happen next, where I was going and with what steps. The future had met me for a moment, a few seconds of living right in it before it flitted to continue moving one bar ahead. During this moment I thought at first I might be toppling from the dock into the sea but it was the feeling, the great feeling so similar to that of my fourth birthday that I thought I was falling forwards on my little bicycle. Pedalling too fast and tipping, with nothing to stop me, over the brow of the hill and down beyond the bench.

The hill was bigger and steeper on the other side and I picked up speed, flying into this new world that opened beneath me until I fell sideways into the grass verge. There was shock and grit and mud but no nettles or foxgloves and when I stood up I could move everything I normally could so knew I had survived the danger that my parents were keeping me from. I was then faced with a terrible decision. I could push my bicycle back up the hill, go home and pretend nothing had happened, or, I could walk a little bit further down the hill and have a closer look at the enormous building there. It wasn't really such a terrible decision and of course I went down the hill.

It was a building from a book. There was a tiny wall around a garden that had untidy grass, many large stones and flowers but no vegetables. A path led to a door so huge it needed a little door cut into it for ordinary people and when I crept inside I could see that this was clearly the house of a giant. There were giants in books who were murderous but there were also those who weren't and either way it didn't look like he was in. I thought about my mother and how she could stretch in here and not touch the ceiling and I wondered why our house wasn't this big. Just inside the doorway there was a giant cup made of stone but I couldn't reach high enough to see what was inside. A giant rug led up the middle of a giant room on either side of which were hundreds of benches, all facing in the same direction where, at the end of the rug, there were steps leading up to his giant bagpipes. O those bagpipes! I still thrill to think of them. I ran towards the tubes that touched the sky and up and around all sorts of delicate wooden protrusions and upholstered froufrou looking for the belly that would catch the breath. I was in the process of climbing upwards when the air was suddenly taken by a magnificent PHOO! I clung on tightly but the PHOO continued and when I brought my other hand to the same level another one joined it, they didn't like each other and became angry. I jumped to the floor and it stopped. Putting my hands in different places made different PHOOs and I knew that this wasn't a set of giant bagpipes after all but a singing xylophone. I sat myself down on the high-backed chair and began to play. The tunes I played on my non-singing xylophone at home, the tunes my father played on his bagpipes – even some of the radio stomping songs. I played happy, angry, silly, excited. I began to play hungry and realised that it was time to go home. Outside my parents were standing waiting, anxious and serious behind the tiny wall.

They didn't speak to me at all but, walking back up the hill, they spoke about me. They worried if anyone had seen me, and if they had, whether they knew who I was, to whom I belonged. There was no need to ask why they hadn't come in, I could see that it wasn't possible and that for reasons that I did not then understand, I shouldn't have been in there either. They carried on talking when we got back to the cottage and they didn't stop when I went to bed. They talked of blood and history and stones that were laid beneath the stones of others; earth and illumination, purpose and meaning. I was happy not to understand everything, I was full of music still and there was no room in me for the dark and the serious.

In the morning my mother told me that I must listen for the bell and watch for the crows that flew when it rang. If the bell had not sounded by noon I could cycle over the hill, past the bench, and play on the organ (the true title of the singing xylophone). Thinking now this generosity was remarkable. I was only just four and still, more or less, eager to do what I was told. They could easily have kept me from my discovery but they didn't. They allowed me to go somewhere where they could not follow and it is only now, after I have seen so many parents seized with jealously over the freedom of their children, that I am truly able to appreciate what a sacrifice this was. My father told me that I had a rare power and to be careful, to run home if I saw another human being.

Day after day I listened for the bells and more often than not I could sit and play until my stomach told me it was time to go home. Sometimes the tunes I wanted to play needed great stretches and I would become exhausted with the effort and need to sit back on the high wooden chair and stare at the black and white in front of me, planning what was to come next. I learned what all the levers did and even the paddles on the floor though I couldn't work both at the same time. I sat back and thought through the tunes that I would make if I ever grew to my mother's proportions. Much of what eventually became the opera *Stairways* was written that way, sitting with my back to the chair, pulling stoppers and pressing pedals in my mind. Every morning and every night I pulled at my fingers to make them grow faster and over time I was able to play more notes at once. As the days grew shorter I had less space to play and would try to make the most of what I had, but sometimes it was so cold my fingers slowed down. Then I would walk about, blowing and rubbing my hands, and in that way came to learn more about the building I played in. The house did belong to a giant but he was invisible and lots of ordinary people came here when he rang the bell that meant I had to stay at home. Sometimes they left things on the rug or there would be new flowers all over. Once, there was an enormous pile of fruit and vegetables and it made me so hungry I couldn't concentrate. My father continued to remind me to run from anyone I saw but I was never given the opportunity. By the door there was a photograph of a crowd, some smiling, some not, and I could see these were the people who I was hiding from. They looked a lot like my mother and father except that they wore strange clothes and were all more or less the same size. Sometimes I would look into their faces and try to guess who they were; I would make up stories about them and play tunes for them. It was a glorious easy time and ended too quickly when I turned from my seat one day to see the crowd, silent, staring and manifest on the long red rug.

Unbeknownst to me I had been the parish scandal for some time. It had started with Ash Granton pegging moles in the top field, hearing music from the church and, thinking it was his neighbour Maric Trent, wandering down to make inquiries on a borrowed cabinet scraper. The music stopped, Maric was nowhere to be seen and Ash urgently wheezed his way back up the hill to the village. When he tracked down Maric in the Black Lion and accused him of playing tricks he discovered the organist had spent the day in the pub with a bevy of witnesses. In wonderment Ash sat with a pint and a pie, forgot about the cabinet scraper and the rumours began. Two weeks later young Virginia Wilson was mooning about the church when the organ began spontaneously to play and she ran terrified away. These first two incidents were reported in the local press and much was made of the haunting magic of the music which pleases me greatly to read now as of course no records survive of these earliest of performances. From these reports the stories spread and grew and spawned others until the matter had nowhere to go but the bishop. Lesser clergy did not have the power to either validate miracles or exorcise organs and one or the other was clearly needed. Bishops, one presumes, are trained in dealing with such matters, and when he made this begrudged visit to the last outpost of his diocese he was perhaps planning to go where no-one else had dared and check the high backed chair for a very small person. He did not get the chance however as even a boy genius in the midst of composition cannot fail to notice an entire parish sneaking up behind him.

CHARLOTTE ALLAN

Considering the fuss I had been causing I should not have been surprised that such a crowd had come to hear me play. These people belonged in a photograph and now they were moving and glaring at me on the rug and when the bishop came at me with his great golden pole I did what any child would do, screamed and ran. As I stumbled across the wooden benches the people began to shout, some of them pushing along the rows to catch me. A large man with no beard leapt out near the giant cup and grabbed me round the middle. I kicked and shouted but he just squeezed tighter and I had to stop before I was crushed to atoms. A lady said, 'Look at his clothes! A proper little pagan,' and a younger one, 'She must be from the side-shows over the way,' then another, 'Is it a boy or a girl?' Someone I couldn't see offered, 'Too short for a girl, too bald for a boy,' and so they laughed chipping in with the likes of 'Who'd have thought it,' and 'Poor filthy thing.' At that moment I remembered what one is advised to do when attacked by a bear, which is to play dead. I relaxed all my muscles and the man was so shocked he dropped me. During the talk and panic over what to do next I took the opportunity to plan my escape. The bishop swooped past muttering 'I see no miracle,' and I followed the path he made with my eyes before springing to my feet and dashing through and past him. The doors were already open and it was easy for me to speed through them, out the garden, over the fence, up the hill and straight into the cottage where I clung to my mother's shin.

An amusing article was written in the local paper and things quickly returned to normal for the normal. When I told my parents everything that had happened they said I would have to stay at home now but that they would try to get me a piano (the next best thing) and would I like a model organ in the meantime that I could use with my imagination? I said it was better than nothing, and indeed it was.

Carousel

PAUL DE HAVILLAND

You're off the plane fast, hand baggage only. You've learned this over the years. You still manage to get a front seat most of the time, but nowadays you have to use more charm than flirt on the check-in girl. You never use the electronic check-in. Where's the joy in selecting your seat with a cursor? Anyway, you suspect those things might hide the best seats.

You can't be in the wrong place because the airport's too small. You remember your phone's been off for the flight and take it from your jacket pocket. Thirty seconds later you're reading a message from Jérémie. He's not able to meet. He gives directions for *le train*. Rendezvous for dinner his house tonight, he will explain. He gives an address. You begin to think you've made a mistake.

You take the train to St Brieuc. There's no flight back till tomorrow so there's not much choice. Jérémie isn't answering his phone, you don't know if you're still invited to stay so you check into a small hotel in the centre. You wish you'd asked to see the room first because it's a 1970s prefabricated fitted suite and it's cream and brown. You console yourself it's clean and the ensuite has a bath. You unpack and go out.

Your guide book trashes St Brieuc but you're pleasantly surprised. You vow, like you do every trip you take, to stop buying guide books. It's a French town, you can get mussels and chips and a *bière pression* so that's what you do. It's a fine hot day so you do this outside in a square almost filled with tables and waiters, and you people-watch as you eat your food and drink your beer. You're British so you haven't mastered how to sit at a café table all afternoon for the price of a cheap meal. You worry someone else might need the table, so you pay the bill and walk.

You're just going to window shop because you don't need anything and you haven't got any space in your flight bag. You buy a gorgeous little sauce boat and a matching cruet set because you never see anything quite like that in Edinburgh, and you've got Peter and Elaine round in a couple of weeks and you need something new for your table setting.

You enjoy the afternoon on your own. You do, really. You're glad on the whole that Jérémie couldn't see you till later because you've only spent a few hours together overall, and a lot of those asleep. An evening will be ideal, you can decide about tomorrow if you hit it off tonight as well as you did in London.

You wonder whether Jérémie regrets inviting you over. It occurs to you he might have been being overly polite, or that maybe in France it is de rigeur to extend such an invitation and for it to be refused.

This thought ruins the rest of the day for you. You go back to the hotel for a bath and to get ready, and consider phoning Jérémie again. You decide against it, but by the time you are ringing his door bell you're wishing you had, convinced you'll be as welcome as Banquo's ghost. But the door buzzes open and you go in.

You climb the stairs of the rambling old house to the top flat. It's one of a few medieval looking buildings dotted here and there in St Brieuc's winding streets, like wonky teeth. A rather handsome, rather young man answers the door. This is not Jérémie, and you immediately conclude you have the wrong place. You start to say, 'Je suis désolé...' but the actually *very* handsome young man smiles and says with only a trace of accent 'Hello. You must be Arthur.' You love the way the French say your name, it almost rehabilitates it for you. Arture. You own up to being Arture, you don't correct his pronunciation.

You see Jérémie come hurriedly down the crooked hall. He places an arm around the handsome young man and reaches his free hand towards yours. 'Ahrthor. So good to see you again. You have found us well?'

'He means easily,' says the man who seems to be the reason Jérémie wasn't at the airport. You reset your expectations for the evening. 'And I'm François.'

You think Jérémie must be paying this boy's college fees or something, then you see François touch Jérémie unselfconsciously as they back away from the door to let you in. You detect love and start to feel more generous, and then think maybe if you were with Jérémie, he might seem like your toy-boy. You think of making an excuse to leave but you realise this would make your disappointment obvious and you've probably caused Jérémie enough of a crisis already.

In the living room you admire the beams holding up the roof and the bold colour scheme and you sit on the couch and Jérémie sits in an armchair. François offers wine, then opens a bottle of Muscadet with waiter-like detachment, asking you about Edinburgh.

You tell him about the New Town and the Old Town, about the theatres and the Cameo cinema where you can take drinks into the auditorium. He likes the word auditorium, it's new to him and he repeats it to get your approval for his pronunciation. He says, 'We must come and visit. It sounds a wonderful city.'

Jérémie says, 'François! We must be invited, perhaps Ahrthor does not like visitors.'

You regret trying to train Jérémie to say Arthur

properly. It was fun at the time, a bit of post coital banter. You say, 'Of course I like visitors. I would love to see you both in Edinburgh.'

You realise that you and Jérémie do not sound like two old friends. You see François realising it too and looking at you. He remains the welcoming host, however, and hands you a glass. The wine is perfect and perfectly chilled. You feel you would like these two under different circumstances. You hope dinner will be over soon.

You strain to remember things about Jérémie and realise you don't know much at all. You can't ask after his mother, she could be dead. You can't ask about his boss because you don't know if he has one. You can't request a viewing of the skiing holiday photos because maybe they don't go skiing, or didn't this year.

You wonder why he was crazy enough to let you come, then you see what must have happened. François got your answer-phone message and Jérémie had no way out. You wonder if it had ever occurred to Jérémie that you would be so stupid as to use the land line number on his card and not the mobile.

François sits down and says, 'We've booked a restaurant. Jérémie told me how much you like Indian food. There is a great restaurant here. It's just down the road so there's no hurry.'

You hate Indian. The very smell of cardamom makes you queasy. But Jérémie would know what you like so there's nothing you can do about it.

François saves the day. You don't know if he does it deliberately but he asks you more questions about Edinburgh, about why you moved to Scotland. You tell him about loving cities, about loving the open country as well and how hard it is to get out of London except for a whole weekend. You tell him you have a boat and how great the sailing is on the Clyde. He says he thought the Clyde was Glasgow so you tell him he's right but it's only two hours from Edinburgh. You don't tell him you moved to be with Gus because Gus has been dead for five years and you don't want to get into all that again.

François says it was so nice you and Jérémie had been able to meet up in London. You say you are often in London visiting friends. François says Jérémie never tells him about his friends. He says he is sorry to interrogate you, but he is trying to catch up a bit. Jérémie says, 'We must go or we will be late for rest-o-ront.'

In the Indian you order things with fruit and coconut and cream and hope there's no cardamom. It's a dead giveaway but you are starting not to care so much after two glasses of Muscadet. You never drink at lunch *and* dinner any more. You order a *grande bière*, because it's half a litre which is like a pint and you're starting to feel homesick.

You're starting to feel sick. Maybe there was cardamom in those potato cakes. You've managed to blether with Jérémie during the starters. You've talked about Tate Britain, where you and Jérémie had admired the Turners. You've begun a promising debate about Turner's love of myth and the Bible but then you blow it when the wine and the beer kicks in and you say to François, 'That's where I first saw Jérémie, captivated by *Agrippina Landing with the Ashes of Germanicus*. It's one of my favourite Turners.'

But François doesn't care about the almost spiritual rendering of Turner's skies. He turns to Jérémie and yells at him and you can't follow the rapid volleys of French in any literal sense, but you think you get the gist.

Now it's just you and Jérémie because François has stormed off, and Jérémie is apologising to you and excusing himself to go to rescue his marriage. You are left with the bill so you pay for a meal no-one has eaten and struggle back to your hotel where you throw up in the handy en suite bath.

Next morning you can't face even the meagre French breakfast, so you drink the hotel's muddy coffee and check out with your flight bag and seven hours to kill until you have to catch a train to the airport.

You walk around a small park and your head starts to clear. You start to long for bacon and eggs and toast because that's the best hangover cure in the world. But, you're in France so the nearest you can find is a place that sells omelettes. It turns out that the omelette and chips are excellent and the coffee is rich and strong and that bacon and eggs has a serious rival.

When you ask for the bill, your mobile bleats and you have a text message. It's Jérémie and he hopes you're still in St Brieuc and can you meet him at a bar he names at 12:30. You're curious and you've got nothing else to do so you text back OK.

That's in twenty minutes so you pay the bill and the waiter gives you directions and you're pleased that your French still works well enough to do this.

On your way you pass a small square where there's a big merry-go-round with old fashioned cars and horses and boats and dolphins for children to ride. There are some boys getting in to one of the cars, and a girl is astride a dolphin. Parents are waving at them and smiling. The ride has a loud sound system blasting out R&B. A voice is singing. You don't take much notice but as you come alongside you can't not hear the lyric and it's 'FUCK WHAT WE HAD, IT DON'T COUNT FOR SHIT NOW!' and no-one's batting an eye-lid, not the parents, not the kids and not the passers by; everyone's as passive as the dolphin the little girl is riding.

And you laugh out loud as you walk along. The lyric gets even more explicit and you look back and the ride has started and the singer's girlfriend is a whore and she's gone down on some other man and the kids are waving and the parents are smiling and waving back and you laugh again. And then you're round the corner and you can see Jérémie, just Jérémie and you know somehow that François doesn't know he's there. Your heart leaps because this can only be an assignation. You see the possibility of having a French lover, of snatched weekends in London when he's there on his frequent business trips.

You want this. You want to break in on this couple and prove you've still got it. You want to fall in love with Jérémie because you need love and he's the only one night stand who's returned your call in five years. You remember when Jérémie left your hotel in London and you said you thought there was something special last night, you said you thought you could fall in love with him. You'd said the same thing your first night with Gus. It's how you check them out. You remember him smiling, and giving you his card and telling you to call. You see him waiting for you now and you think he must have meant it.

You make a decision.

You see you're full of crap. He's just there to plead with you to never call again. You turn back and walk past the roundabout and as you do the song is building back to the 'Fuck what we had, it don't count for shit now!' chorus and you join in and sing along at the top of your voice.

The Doll Factory

HEATHER RICHARDSON

Brigadier H. Multhavy
Department of Post-Combat Therapeutic Support
Ministry of Defence (UK Sector)
London
SW365 53NC
23 May 2093

Dear Doctor Hibbert

Re. Anne Sullivan

Thank you for you letter regarding your patient. As you say, it is a most distressing case, particularly as the children were so young. It is regrettable that the press coverage focused with such intensity on Miss Sullivan's military background. I am enclosing the bulk of the file re. Former Combatant 000174329. I trust these few items will help you develop a treatment regime for Miss Sullivan.

Although Former Combatant 000174329's case is in many ways different from Miss Sullivan's, particularly in respect of his having undergone spontaneous rehumanisation, it is interesting that they served in the same unit, and in both cases the imminent crisis appears to have been flagged up by lapses in the individual's protective amnesia. This may be a useful indicator in our future follow-up of Former Combatants. I am enclosing the draft version of a study due to be published in the *European Journal of Psychiatry* later this year, which may be of interest.

The items found at Former Combatant 000174329's last known address may be no more than curiosities, but I am including them nonetheless. Miss Sampson's story, while clearly plagiarism of sorts, appears to *pre-date* Anne Sullivan's actions.

I should be grateful if you would update me on Miss Sullivan's progress. In cases such as these we should be able to overcome the traditional boundaries between our departments, for the benefit of our patients.

Yours sincerely

Brigadier H. Multhavy

Encs.

COMBINED MILITARY OF THE NORTH ATLANTIC

Job Sheet

Date of engagement: 12/29/2090

Location of engagement: Central Combat Zone,
                                 Location Code ZAG/18-35

Unit: Infantry Sub-Unit 16/543

Details of engagement:
Unit made covert approach to Revos settlement identified by
sat. recon. Engaged with and eliminated Revos active unit.

Enemy casualties/fatalities: 52

Prisoners taken: 0

Military casualties/fatalities: 0

Job Sheet completed by (name/rank/no.):
J. Garvey/Serg./000101534

COMBINED MILITARY OF THE NORTH ATLANTIC

Behavioural Alert Form

Date and time of incident: 12/29/90 19.00hrs (approx)

Location: Doll Factory #135 (Periph. Central Zone)

Combatant Serial No(s): 000174329

Details of incident:
Infantry Sub-Unit 16/543 visited the Doll Factory for statutory recreation following active service in Central Combat Zone. Unit first entered so-called 'Rape Room'. Combatant 000174329 left room after approx 10 minutes. Tech-worker Henricks offered Combatant 000174329 a private room with the Doll spec. of his choice. Combatant 000174329 reportedly stated that he 'wanted love.' Tech-worker Henricks supplied a Doll programmed for affection. CC playback shows no recreation took place, although combatant 000174329 lay in Doll's arms.

? spontaneous rehumanisation

Reported by:
Alexi Krechinov, S'visor Doll Factory #135

CMNA Office use only

Date Received: 1/5/91 **Risk grade:** 3

Action code: W/A

Received by (name/rank/no.):
P. Ramesh/Lieut/000103624

COMBINED MILITARY OF THE NORTH ATLANTIC

PSYCHIATRIC MEDICAL REPORT ON
COMBATANT 000174329

DATE OF REPORT: **2/28/91**

NAME OF DOCTOR: **BRIG. H MULTHAVY**

The patient (referred to as C) was referred to the Department
of Post-Combat Therapeutic Support following a report of
deviant behaviour while on active service in the Central
Combat Zone. The objective of the consultation was to
establish whether so-called 'spontaneous rehumanisation' had
taken place, and to assess C's capacity for further military duty.

Demeanour
C was neatly groomed. His uniform was clean and pressed.
He was pale and appeared to be exhausted. His manner was
anxious and withdrawn, his speech quiet and hesitant. It was
noted that his fingernails had been bitten to such an extent
that the nail bed was exposed. He was keen to co-operate
with the medical team, but expressed a fear that he might say
the 'wrong thing'.

History
C was born on 17 May 2070. His father was a soldier, but had
left the family home when C was around 2 years old. He
described his relationship with his mother as loving and
affectionate. C had an older half-sister, who he had been close
to, describing her as his 'mini-mum'. However, mother and
daughter became estranged during the girl's late teens, and at
the time of the consultation C had not seen his half-sister for
nearly 10 years. C's mother died of skin cancer when he was
16, and he joined the army shortly after. He had attempted to
locate his half-sister during his mother's final illness, in the

hope of effecting a reconciliation, but had been unable to find her. This had caused him considerable guilt at the time, and was still a source of regret to him.

Service Record
After basic training C served for 18 months in a support battalion, before applying for an active service unit. Psych. reports carried out as part of the selection process found no evidence of instability or underlying mental disorder. C was assessed to be of slightly below average intelligence. There is no history of disciplinary problems. On selection for an active service unit C was implanted with a subcutaneous depo containing CombatReadi®, and signed a consent form indicating he understood the implications.

Background to incident
C had served with his active service unit for around 2 years at the time of the incident. As is usual with CombatReadi® subjects, he has little memory of specific military operations from this period. He confirmed that following his implant he felt 'cool-headed', and less subject to impulsive behaviour. As he put it, 'I might still get angry or afraid, but I could store it up until I was out of the Combat Zone.' On the night of the incident that appeared to precipitate his breakdown, he experienced some anxiety while observing an enemy encampment. In his own words he 'felt bad' about what the unit were about to do, especially as there were women and children in the camp. These feelings intensified during the engagement. C experienced a particular feeling of antipathy towards a female member of the unit. He refused to give details of her actions, saying only she had been 'more crueller (sic) than she had to be.' C confirmed that he could *remember* exactly what had happened during the engagement, but would not share his recollections with me. After the engagement the unit proceeded to a so-called 'Doll Factory' for statutory recreation. C found his feeling of distress

intensifying in the so-called 'rape room' where units customarily spend their first period of recreation. He confirmed that he understood the 'girls' were in fact artificial humans, and therefore unable to experience fear or pain. He said he felt an unbearable longing for affection and reassurance, and feared that if he didn't leave the room he would die.

Current symptoms
Following the incident C was withdrawn from active service and returned to the UK for observation and assessment. Blood tests indicate that levels of CombatReadi® in his system were abnormally low, indicating that the drug had been eliminated more quickly than is usual. On removal, there was no sign of any fault with the depo. C confirmed that he has experienced flashbacks and nightmares, has found his concentration impaired and his appetite diminished. He has no close relationships. When questioned about suicidal thoughts he became agitated and uncooperative.

Conclusion and recommendations
The term 'Spontaneous Rehumanisation' is often used for cases such as these, but in my opinion it is not helpful. For reasons not yet understood C's response to CombatReadi® was only partially successful. He displays several symptoms of Post-Traumatic Stress Disorder (PTSD), and as such is no longer fit for active service. Experience with other former combatants has shown that even with intensive psychotherapy and medication for depression/anxiety, it is unlikely that C will be suitable to fulfil any role in the military, and therefore I would recommend his case be processed for immediate medical retirement.

28 February 2091

INCIDENCE OF POST-TRAUMATIC STRESS DISORDER IN
SUBJECTS TREATED WITH MILITARY-SPECIFIC
PSYCHOTROPIC DRUGS

CHRISTINA MANN, FRCPsych
MICHAEL PAINTER, FRCPsych

Department of Combat Medicine, Kings College London

Declaration of Interest: Funded by European Medical Research Council

INTRODUCTION

Post-Traumatic Stress Disorder was an occupational hazard for combatants in the 20th and much of the 21st centuries. The introduction of military-specific psychotropic drugs such as CombatReadi®, with its effects of protective dissociation, impulse control and the so-called 'moral psychopath paradox', has all but eradicated this scourge of military service. The delivery method of such drugs has commonly been a subcutaneous slow-release depo, with an average life of 5-6 years. Combatants treated with CombatReadi® have significantly improved mental health outcomes post military service, with lower incidence of suicide, alcohol/drug abuse and relationship failure as compared with previous generations of combatants. However, during the war of the last decade, there have been a number of reports of drug failure, and so-called 'spontaneous rehumanisation'.

METHOD

Case studies of 15 combatants who had experienced symptoms of PTSD or manifested deviant behaviour were analysed for areas of commonality. Incidence of PTSD was confirmed using Horowitz's Impact of Event (IES),

Speilberger's State Anxiety (SANX) and the Peri-Traumatic Dissociation Questionnaire (PDEQ).

Subjects then underwent a psychiatric assessment identical to the one that they had originally undergone before being accepted into an active service unit, to identify changes in their mental health profile. Each subject also engaged in a series of consultations with the report authors, using hypnotherapy and regression, to identify symptoms of 'spontaneous rehumanisation'.

RESULTS

The results of the repeated psych. tests reveal significant changes in the mental well being of the subjects. Typical changes included: increased anxiety and fearfulness, a sense of impending 'judgement' and in some cases a tendency towards impulsive behaviour and violence towards self or others. Five subjects confirmed they had attempted suicide. Two admitted violent acts towards others, particularly close family members. (See Fig. 1)

Symptoms or warning signs of 'spontaneous rehumanisation' included sudden disgust at combat in general and fellow unit members in particular, empathy with the enemy, distress over the death of enemy women and children, and generalised feelings of fearfulness. All subjects expressed their self-disgust at what they perceived as their 'betrayal' of their unit. (See Fig. 2)

CONCLUSIONS

The new-generation military-specific psychotropic drugs have revolutionised mental health outcomes for combatants, and are generally well tolerated with a low side-effect profile. However, on occasion the drugs appear to be eliminated from some individuals more quickly than expected, with damaging results both to their fitness for service and their long-term well-being. Given the small sample of subjects in this study it is not yet possible to identify characteristics that may predispose combatants to 'spontaneous rehumanisation'. Long term retrospective studies are recommended to enable military medical staff to screen out such vulnerable individuals and bar them from active service units.

A Soldiers Story

By
[XXXXXXX XXXXX]

I always wanted to be a soldier from when I was little, but the stuff that happened in the Doll Factory changed that. We were on a really tough engagement at a town where the revos were holed up, and the problem is they recruit women and even kids now, so you can't trust any of them even if they look like civilians. When it was over Sarge said we had earned a visit to the Doll Factory, that's what we always do after a bad one. We got there and we were still all dirty, and the first thing they do at the Doll Factory is you get shown to the rape room. They have a few girls there, well I call them girls but obviously they are artificial humans so not really getting hurt but it doesn't seem that way because they are really realistic. In the rape room they make the girls look like the woman from the revo towns because they reckon that gets it all out of our system and that way we won't do it for real and be had up for war crimes. After the rape room you get to have a shower and then get a private room for half an hour, you can choose what you want the girl programmed like, scared or horny or a fighter or whatever. Some guys save up their pay and take a pic of the girlfriends they had at home before they joined up and the techs at the Doll Factory adapt one of the girls specially but it costs a fortune

57

and anyway I'd never had anyone really, I was only 16 when I joined up. So this time we went into the rape room and I couldn't face it. Sullivan was the worst, I've never seen anyone act so cruel and some people would be surprised that a woman would act that way to another girl even if she was an artificial human, but all I say is you don't need a dick to rape a girl. Something just snapped in my head and I went out and one of the techs said, what's wrong?, and said he'd get me a girl, and what did I want?, and I just said I want love I want love. I can't remember much after that but next I know I'm talking to the shrink and he said to write it down, it might help, but I didn't remember much then. I can now, that's why I'm writing this. After I saw the shrink I got my discharge papers, and I think people should know what is happening in the army to the ordinary soldier.

THE END

Frozen North

The Magazine of Quality Fiction

25 January 2092

Dear [XXXXXX XXXXX]

Re. 'A Soldier's Story'

Thank you for your submission to Frozen North. We receive a great many submissions of very high quality, and I regret that on this occasion we will not be publishing your story.

Yours faithfully

Anita Sampson
Editor

Frozen North Publications, 18 Deansgate, Leicester, LE2 3XK

Issue 16, Autumn 2092   *Killing Zone*

The Doll Factory Trinity

ANITA SAMPSON

1) Engagement

This was the best way to kill Revos, that's what Sergeant Grove always said. On the sneak, working your way through the darkness surrounding the settlement, looking out for the lookouts. Alton was partnered with O'Reilly for this engagement. It gave him a bad feeling. O'Reilly was one vicious bitch.

They were so close they could see in through the windows of the houses. Alton watched a dark-haired woman walk across a room, carrying a sleeping child. A dim light came on in the next room, glowing through the curtains. Alton imagined the woman laying the child down in bed, tucking the covers in. He froze for a moment, panicked by that alien sense of empathy. *Enemies,* he reminded himself. *They're all enemies.*

O'Reilly was by his side, her breathing coming fast and shallow. He touched his earpiece just as Sergeant Grove gave the order, one whispered word transmitted to every one of them at precisely the same second. *Now.*

They ran forward towards the houses. Alton kicked in the door of the house he'd been watching and fired at the group of men hunched around the kitchen table. O'Reilly was in after him, chasing after one who had run towards the back door. Alton thought he'd got all of the others, but one was only wounded. The injured man pulled a handgun from his belt and fired a wild shot in O'Reilly's direction. The bullet brushed her shoulder as she turned from killing the would-be runner. 'For fuck's sake Alton,' she yelled, letting loose a half-dozen rounds into the man. She walked forward and lifted the handgun from the dead man's hand, then turned to glare at Alton. 'You could have got me killed you dumb fuck.'

'Let's go,' Alton said. 'We're done here.'

O'Reilly frowned. 'What are you talking about? We haven't cleared the house.' She nodded towards the closed bedroom door. 'I'll go in. You cover me.'

They walked as quietly as they could towards the door and positioned themselves one on either side. O'Reilly nodded and quickly turned to kick the door open. Alton moved behind her, his gun pointed at the dark-haired woman who was standing against the far wall. Alton couldn't see any sign of the child. *Under the bed,* he thought, but said nothing. 'Hang fire,' O'Reilly said. Alton realised he'd been holding his breath. He lowered his gun.

'Yeah,' he said. 'She's not armed. Let's leave her.'

O'Reilly looked at him like he was crazy. 'You really are a dumb fuck. We're not leaving her. Let's have some fun first.'

'That's against regulations. We can go to the Doll Factory afterwards, Sarge said so.'

'To hell with the Doll Factory. I want a real one to hurt.' O'Reilly pushed him out of the room. 'You wait for me. And if you ever grass me up...' She slammed the door in his face.

Alton held his hands over his ears, but he couldn't block out the woman's screaming. It seemed to go on for a long time, and then, at last, the blessed release of two gunshots. O'Reilly came out of the room. One of her hands was dark with blood. 'What do ya know,' she said cheerfully. 'There was a kid in there too. Hiding under the bed.' She shook her head. 'Two for the price of one, eh?'

O'Reilly sat beside him in the APC as they moved out of the zone. The vehicle lurched over the rough terrain and her leg nudged against his. He could feel the heat of her body. She smelt of blood. They all did.

2) The Doll Factory

The industrial estate seemed deserted. The APC drove along the long straight road past dark warehouses and empty office blocks. At last it pulled in to the car park at the front of a windowless hangar. The one door was heavily reinforced and watched over by a security camera. Sergeant Grove typed a code into the keypad beside the door and it opened.

Inside was a dusty reception area. A stocky man sat behind a Perspex security screen. He buzzed another door open. Sergeant Grove led them through, down a brightly lit corridor. A tech-worker met them and beckoned them to follow him. The corridor turned and ended in another locked door. 'Thirty minutes,' the tech-worker said, using a keycard to unlock the door.

There were six girls in the room. They stood huddled together in the corner, looking fearfully at the soldiers. From this distance they looked real. It was only when you got closer that you became aware of the impossible flawlessness of their skin. They were dark-haired, like the Revos women, dressed like them too. Traditional music from the Central Zone played through speakers set high on the walls.

'What are you waiting for?' Sergeant Grove roared. 'We've only got thirty minutes. Get to it.'

The men advanced on the girls, who clung on to each other. One of them was sobbing. She was pulled out first by two of the older guys. They dragged her across the room to one of the old mattresses that lay on the floor. Her sobbing intensified as they pushed her down and began tearing at her clothes.

Alton became aware that O'Reilly was staring at him. 'What's your problem?' she said coldly. 'You're acting like a fucking padre.' The rest of the Unit were on the girls now, punching them, slapping their faces, forcing them onto their knees. O'Reilly reached into her pocket and pulled out her fingerstall. Alton had seen it too many times before. O'Reilly had made it specially. She'd stitched it from old boot-leather. It covered the length of her index finger and was covered with sharp studs. As she fastened it on Alton noticed that the blood on it looked fresh. 'Come on then,' she said. 'I want you to hold one down for me.'

Alton felt light-headed. The harsh glare of the strip lighting seemed to pound against his eyes and the room had become airless. He struggled to take a breath, but his lungs were tight. Stumbling, he found his way to the door and half-fell out into the corridor.

He stood there for a moment, leaning against the wall. His legs were trembling. *Battle-shock*, he thought, and then remembered he shouldn't be suffering from battle-shock. They'd told him that, when he signed up for the Unit, and had the depo implanted under the skin of his upper arm. A five year dose of CombatReadi® meant you could cope with anything, and afterwards, when it wore off, it was as if you'd never seen active service. No PTSD, no nightmares, nothing. That's what they'd told him.

A tech-worker approached him cautiously. 'Okay mate?'

Alton stared at the man. He tried to form his lips into a reply, but no words came out.

'Let me get you a private room mate,' the tech-worker said. 'What sort of girl you want? Nympho-girl? Big cuddly mama?'

Alton staggered, as if the floor had buckled under him. At last he could speak. 'I want love,' he said. 'I want love.'

63

3) Peacetime

Alton stowed the mop and bucket in the cupboard, took off his overalls and left the office block. Six years now since he'd been discharged from the Unit. He had his army pension, for what it was worth. This cleaning job topped it up so he could afford his rent. It wasn't much of a job, but it suited him just fine. He worked alone through the early hours, which was the worst time for the thoughts. Better to be here, scrubbing away the filth of the day than to be lying alone in his bed-sit, thinking, remembering…

He said goodbye to the security guy on the front desk and walked out of the office block. The morning air smelt fresh and cool. A few of the office workers were arriving now, keen to impress someone.

There was a café on his way home. He stopped there every morning for some tea and toast. They knew him there, knew he didn't want to talk. He settled himself at an empty table and pulled his notebook from his pocket. Every day it seemed he remembered something else. The shrink had said it would be good for him to write it all down. He couldn't see how it would help, but he'd started doing it, and now he couldn't stop. He'd filled three notebooks so far.

The door of the café opened and a woman came in, pushing a buggy. The child was asleep, chin tucked down onto his chest. The woman bent over to recline the buggy seat. That was when Alton realised it was O'Reilly. Her hair was no longer cropped short and her body had filled out. Looking more closely Alton saw that she was pregnant. Maybe six months gone. Alton stared at her, panic fluttering in his chest. They weren't meant to meet up, that was one of the conditions of serving in the Unit. O'Reilly looked up, met his eye. He saw her confusion, then the recognition. 'Jesus, Alton! What

Issue 16, Autumn 2092　　　　　　　　*Killing Zone*

happened to you? You look...'

'Why are you here?' His voice sounded hoarse.

'Between trains.'

'You left the Army?'

'Did my five, got out alive.' The child stirred in his sleep, stretched one arm up above his head and relaxed again. O'Reilly smiled down at him.

'How can you have this life?' Alton said. 'After what you've done.'

O'Reilly frowned. 'What do you mean? We killed people, that was our job.'

'But you,' Alton struggled to get a breath. 'You were so cruel.'

'What are you talking about?' O'Reilly's face was blank. She didn't remember.

'Here.' He threw his notebook down on the table in front of her. 'Read this. Read what you did. See if you deserve to be...' He glanced once more at the sleeping child and remembered a different boy, rocked to sleep by his dark-haired mother in another place, another time.

Alton stumbled out of the café into the morning. The daylight seemed too bright to him, as harsh as strip lighting. He broke into a run, fleeing the light. He had to find a place to hide. Somewhere dark, where justice couldn't find him.

Tokes from the Wild

TYLER KEEVIL

The bus ride to Rick's hometown costs fifty bucks and lasts about eight hours. We're giddy as kids going to day camp for the first ninety minutes or so. Then the excitement wears off, conversation dries up, and we end up staring out the windows. Even the countryside is boring – an endless panorama of flat, burnt-out fields and barren hillsides. I pull out the hunting knife my parents got me, showing off for Rick.

'Sweet, man,' he says. 'What are you gonna do with that?'

'Stab some bears.'

Rick grins. He has shoulder-length hair and a full beard, a rarity in our grade. Except for his tie-dyed shirts and tattered cords, he looks a bit like Jesus. We're not exactly best friends – he's lived in Prince George most of his life and only came down to Vancouver to finish high school. I was a little surprised when he invited me to go tree planting and stay with his family. We were both drunk, and at a party. I think he was a little surprised when I accepted.

Halfway there the bus stops at a greasy spoon diner for a food break. We pour out onto the hot pavement, a mixed bag of people too old or too young or too poor to drive themselves. While the others file inside, Rick asks me if I want to smoke some weed. I've always been a bit of a chicken about pot but I tell him I'll go with him. We sneak behind the diner; he magically produces his pipe and sparks it. The smoke hangs sweetly in the heat.

'This is going to be great,' Rick assures me, casually exhaling. 'I've never done it before, either – but my dad says tree planting rules. We'll make wicked money.'

'Sure,' I agree.

I'm still too chicken to smoke any.

★

At the bus depot we're picked up by a middle-aged, frizzy-haired woman driving a station wagon: Rick's mom. Miranda gives me a tour of Prince George on the way to their house, which is a few miles out of town. Rick keeps rolling his eyes, obviously embarrassed, but I like her. She seems cheerful, weary, and completely unassuming.

She tells me: 'The town might not look like much, but it's home.'

Everything is flat in Prince George – a collection of strip malls and bungalows and squat apartment buildings. On the edge of town we pass through an area of run-down stucco houses with untended yards. I catch glimpses of illegible graffiti, broken windows, a snarl of old wire fencing. Miranda shakes her head, clucking sadly.

'This is the Indian Reserve,' she tells me.

'Oh,' I say, as if that explains everything.

At the next corner two Native children are playing hopscotch, grinning madly, their tanned skin gleaming in the sun.

★

Over pasta and meat sauce that night I meet the rest of Rick's family. His dad, Fred, is a big, balding bushman who burps and farts at the table. Fred's a contractor for the forestry companies. I learn that he's the one who sold Clayton – our boss – the tree planting contracts we'll be working on. Then there's Neil, the brother, who looks like a younger version of Rick. He dresses the same, but can't quite grow a full beard.

Sorrel's my favourite. Rick's sister is five or six. She seems out of place among the rest of the clan: she's the only one with blonde hair and doesn't take after her mother or father. When introduced she manages a shy smile and says nothing, but throughout the meal I catch her sneaking discreet glances at me, sizing me up as a potential friend.

'This sure is tasty,' I say.

Everybody nods politely.

After dinner Neil takes me outside to show me his dirt bike. He hops on, twisting the throttle until my ears ache and a cloud of smoke surrounds us like noxious gas.

'Ain't it great?' he shouts.

I give him the thumbs up. He peels out of the drive, not quite in control, and whines off down the road. I don't expect our relationship to go much further than that.

*

Their house is a renovated cabin with no room for new bodies. Rick and I sleep in a massive canvas tent on the front lawn. Inside, there's a pot-bellied stove, a dirty rug, an old sofa and two cots. I feel like I'm on safari. Rick's parents are charging me ten bucks a day and fifteen for the weekends. I'm not used to paying to stay at a friend's house but Rick's not quite my friend and the fee includes food, so I guess that makes it fair.

I arrange my things and get out my dad's old Walkman. He gave it to me as a going away present, along with his collection of battered tapes, instead of the mp3 player I asked for. I crank up the volume, sprawling out on the sofa, wishing I had something to read. The springs creak and groan as I shift around, trying to get comfortable. I'm on the second side of *Harvest* when Rick comes in and asks me if I want to smoke some pot.

'I don't really feel like it,' I tell him, feeling guilty.

I listen to him sucking on his pipe outside the tent.

*

'Jesus Christ,' Rick moans, stamping his feet.

We're standing at the roadside in front of Rick's house, shivering, dressed in army pants, plaid shirts, gardening gloves and hiking boots. It doesn't feel like summer; the morning murk is cold and clammy. Drowsy from lack of sleep, we wait in miserable silence for the sun to rise or for Clayton to arrive – whichever comes first.

Headlights appear at the end of the road. A Ford truck with rusty hubcaps rattles to a stop in front of us. We toss our gear in the back and hop in the cab to meet our boss.

Clayton's got a baseball hat on his head and a can of beer in his hand. When he grins it looks like a sneer because of an obvious harelip. As soon as we're settled he starts laying into us – calling us rookies and city slickers and bed-wetters.

'I've lived up here my whole life,' Rick protests.

'The city's made you soft. What a couple of greenhorns.'

He only shuts up about it to swill from his morning beer. When the beer's finished, he starts fishing around in the glove box. He pulls out a pipe and a sack of weed and packs the pipe while he drives.

'Hope you rookies are ready to work. Us three are the only crew today.'

He sparks, inhales, and thrusts the smouldering bowl at me.

Rick says, 'He doesn't smoke.'

'What the fuck?'

'Sure I do.' I snatch up the pipe before the storm hits. 'Once in a while.'

I sense Rick's eyes boring into me as I puff on the pipe. I want to tell him that I'm not inhaling, but I guess it wouldn't make much difference.

For him, I didn't even bother to pretend.

★

Tree planting is simple.

You're given a shovel and a belt with two sacks that dangle from your hips like giant holsters. You load the sacks with yearlings – baby trees – and head out to your allotted portion of forest. You stick the shovel in the ground, open a hole, drop in the tree – making sure the roots are good and deep – and press the hole closed with your boot. Depending on the terrain and what you're planting, you've just made anywhere from five to thirty-five cents. Then you do it again. And again. And again.

By the end of the first day my hands are raw with blisters that have popped and oozed, it hurts to walk from stomping on the shovel, and I'm so covered in bug bites I look like I'm suffering from some strange disease. I've made about thirty bucks. Once I deduct my camp costs and Clayton's equipment rental, I'm breaking just about even.

Tree planting is simple, but not easy.

★

Clayton drops us off, already on his third beer, and tells us we did okay for a couple of greenhorns. He says it sardonically but I'm grateful for any scrap of respect.

'Be ready on time tomorrow because we gotta pick up the rest of the crew.'

Neither of us points out that we were the ones waiting for him this morning.

Rick and I doze our way through dinner, managing to answer any polite questions that come our way. Fred ribs

Rick for planting less trees than me, but Rick barely cracks a smile. After we wash up he tells me he's going to buy some beers. He doesn't invite me along but by that point I'm too tired to care. I collapse on my cot. I never want to move again. The thought of getting up tomorrow morning nauseates me. I want to phone my parents, tell them I'm through. Nobody will really care if I do – but in my heart I'll always know my first big adventure was a failure. I turn my face into the cushions, fighting tears, wishing I could just grow a set of wings and fly away.

'Are you okay?'

I look up, rubbing hurriedly at my eyes. Sorrel's at the tent door. I manage a weak smile, relieved that it's her who's caught me acting like a baby.

'Sure. I hurt my hands today, that's all.'

I hold them out so she can see the open sores.

'I'll get you my cartoon band-aids,' she promises. 'That's what I use.'

She brings me the plasters and helps me put them on. She concentrates very hard on placing the brightly coloured strips carefully over my blisters, getting the angle just right. Bent over my hands, her blonde head is a tangle of twigs, grass, and hopeless snarls. At that moment I'm certain she's a changeling.

'I'm going to be a nurse,' she says.

★

Five of us squeeze into the truck the next morning.

The two new crew members are Annie and Walter. Annie's got dreadlocks and the well-muscled arms of a seasoned planter. A grinning Bob Marley adorns the front of her T-shirt. Walter is Clayton's friend from way back. He's strange and soft-spoken with a pinched, rodent's face. When he does speak it's difficult to understand him because he's missing five front teeth from the top row. Just before we arrive on site he lights a joint. I puff at it tentatively, still faking my inhales, hoping I don't look like the amateur I am. The cab becomes a giant hot box. When we open the doors to get out clouds of smoke follow us like ghosts.

I shove trees in my sacks and head for the woods, hoping the second day won't be as bad as the first. It's not. It's worse. Sorrel's bandages wear off in minutes and my hands start to bleed. I can barely hold my shovel. I know I'm not going to plant enough to cover camp costs. By lunch, I'm so miserable that I forget not to inhale when the half-time joint comes my way. After two or three tokes I feel better. Much better. I stand up. The sun is very bright and the trees are very green and the air smells very fresh. Clayton's looking at me. They're all looking at me. Rick asks me how I feel.

Great. I feel great.

They snicker at my virgin-high, but I don't care.

The rest of the day is much easier, and the rest of the week.

*

On Friday Clayton takes Rick and I out to a bar in Prince George. The carpet smells like sour beer and the walls are decorated with ice hockey sticks, jerseys, and other sports memorabilia. Clayton's warming to us, finally. He buys me my first pint, telling me I've earned the rookie of the week award by planting more trees than Rick. I see Rick's expression and try to make light of it by changing the subject. First we talk hockey, then we talk movies, and by that point Clayton's pretty hammered.

'I cheat on my wife,' he tells us.

'You're married?'

'Yeah. But I go pig-fucking sometimes. Got one chick pregnant.'

He explains that pig-fucking involves picking the biggest, ugliest girl in a bar and taking her home for the night.

I can't get a line on his tone. It's part boast, part confession – he's proud and ashamed at the same time. I wash it all down with more beer, trying to figure it out, trying not to judge him.

I hear more about Clayton from Rick's mom while we're doing the dishes one night. She tells me he wasn't always a drunk, didn't always act like he does. In school he wrote plays and got all the other kids to perform them. He even won an essay-writing contest.

'Clayton?' I ask. 'Are you kidding?'

'I used to volunteer at the school. Everybody adored him.'

'What happened?'

'There was an accident. A car crash. After that…'

She shakes her head, places the last cup gently on the draining board.

*

Sorrel's teaching herself to ride a bike. She doesn't have training wheels and nobody wants to help her so all weekend I end up jogging along behind her, balancing the bike by the back of its seat. She wears Neil's dirt bike helmet for protection. It's too big and keeps slipping over her eyes, but she seems to be learning quickly.

'Okay, ready?'

'Go!'

Once she gets up a head of steam, handlebar streamers snapping in the wind, she tells me to let go. I do, and she immediately wipes out in the gravel. She hops up and starts kicking the bike, the helmet bobbing crazily on her head. Her knees are skinned and bloody; tears of rage stream down her cheeks. Once she wears herself out she picks up the bike and gets back on.

'Well?' she demands, looking back at me. 'Aren't we going again?'

That night I wonder if I could convince my parents to adopt her.

★

Our next contract is for a plot of land an hour from Prince George. Clayton's arranged to have us all stay at a nearby campground. Walter drives his own car so we can pick up a new crew member along the way. Brady's our age, with a smooth, feminine face and wild blue eyes. The first thing he says to me is, 'You're a city-sucker, huh? I can tell by your eyes. They've gone all slanty from hanging around so many chinks.'

Clayton finds that hilarious. With Brady around it's worse than day one. All of a sudden I'm the butt of every joke, and when they're not ridiculing me the racist remarks are flying. Their favourite insults are chink and chug and raghead and nipper.

I keep my mouth shut and my head down.

The only good thing about the new place is where we sleep. Instead of tents Clayton's rented a battered aluminium trailer for the crew to share. Rick and I take the double room, isolating Brady. This pisses him off even more, makes him like me even less. Before dinner on the first night, the rest of the crew goes off to smoke up and hackey-sack, but I'm sick of the mockery and stay behind.

'He wants to jerk off,' Brady taunts.

Everybody laughs. I wonder if I'll have to fight him eventually.

★

Clayton and his wife stay in a separate trailer, which doubles as our mess hall. Over dinner Clayton tells us about the girl on his crew who got mauled by a grizzly the previous summer. She was listening to her Walkman and didn't hear

75

the bear until it was right on top of her.

'Practically tore her head off. All those fuckers who want to ban bear hunting should have seen what it did to that girl.' He glances at his wife. 'Right, babe?'

His wife nods in demure agreement, serves up another helping of sloppy Joes. The meat is chewy and smells strange. She's not as good a cook as Rick's mom but she's prettier. Looking at her, I find Clayton and his pig-fucking even more bewildering.

I ask Rick about Clayton's accident as we're getting ready for bed. He doesn't know much, but he knows Walter was driving. They were both our age. Clayton had a scholarship to Simon Fraser University – the same place I'm applying. He never went.

'I don't think he had the head for it after that.'

'What – you mean his brain got messed up?'

Rick shrugs. 'He just wasn't the same.'

I drift off thinking about Walter's missing teeth, wondering if they got knocked out in the crash. Maybe that's why he's never bothered to get them fixed.

*

Brady and Clayton are convinced that the Chinese are taking over Canada. They explain their elaborate theories to me on the way to and from the planting ground.

'Sure,' Brady says. 'They come into Vancouver, get settled, then fly all their relatives in. Pretty soon there'll be more of them than us.'

'Amen, brother. A-fucking-men.' Clayton's features twist as he struggles to hold in his lungful of smoke. 'And next they bring in their drugs, set up their gangs. What a gong-show. We wouldn't have half the drug problems if it wasn't for the chinks.'

Brady's never been to the city, and Clayton's only been once. All he remembers is the tall buildings and the junkies on Hastings Street. I try to think of something that will torpedo their racism without making me the target of more ridicule.

'There's some pretty cool Chinese people, too.'

'Chink-lover,' Brady says, blowing smoke in my face.

★

My only refuge is the forest.

Nobody can touch me there. I just plant and plant and I do it better and better each day. I've become a machine, running on a steady supply of marijuana. My totals are climbing. The only one who plants more than me is Clayton, and he's a veteran, a highballer. I feel bad for Rick, who's been desperately trying to keep up. I've even considered lying to him about my totals, but it's no good because Clayton gets us to announce them in front of everybody at the end of each day.

I'm in the woods, thinking about that, when I hear a snorting and pawing and grunting coming from a cluster of trees. I put a hand to the knife tucked in my belt and start singing at the top of my lungs. Clayton's told me to make noise if I come across a bear. The snorting gets louder. The bushes are shaking. I turn, getting ready to run. There's a wild cry and the snapping of branches and Brady appears, busting his gut laughing. I shake my head, feeling like I could stab him.

At camp everybody loves it.

'So the rookie fell for it!'

There's lots of laughter at my expense.

'Once a city-sucker, always a city-sucker,' Rick declares.

I look at him oddly. He's got the decency to look away, at least.

★

I haven't needed to read his mind to sense Rick's growing resentment. Around the others we keep up pretences. Alone, in our room, we're silent. I listen to my music and read dime store paperbacks that I've found in the trailer – pure escapism. Rick hacky-sacks by himself or pretends to sleep. Sometimes I try to pinpoint when things turned sour between us, but it all seems childish and petty and strange.

Usually, Rick's the last to quit each day – frantically trying to top up his total – so when I go to reload my sacks on Wednesday afternoon I'm surprised to find him lounging by the boxes of yearlings, his planting gear strewn about him. It's only two o'clock.

'How you doing?' he asks me.

'All right. You?'

He yawns dramatically. His gesture takes in the equipment, the baby trees, and the surrounding forest.

'I'm all through with this.'

*

Fred picks him up the next day. Nobody else understands. I don't really, either. It's one thing to be competitive. It's something else entirely to just quit, especially when your father's the contractor. I try to imagine explaining it to my own dad, but I can't.

'Shitty for you, man,' Clayton tells me. 'Come all the way up here, then have your buddy sell out on you like that. That's tough.'

Oddly enough it changes things for the better. Clayton eases off on me, partly out of sympathy and partly because he can't afford to lose another crew member. At the same time, Brady gets distracted by Annie. Instead of bullying me he starts chasing after her. Ironically, he likes having me there while he flirts with her. I guess it takes the pressure off. The three of us just hang around, smoking and drinking and badmouthing Rick. Camp life becomes suddenly pleasant.

Annie sells me my own bag of weed. At the end of each night, I lock myself in my room, light a joint, and listen to my dad's old tapes.

The hours pass, and the days, in a hazy, almost hallucinatory fog.

★

On weekends we abandon camp.

Everybody else gets to go home, but I'm forced to stay at Rick's. He's sleeping in his old room, now – the farce of his independence having fallen apart. Fred and Miranda treat me politely, if a little coldly. Nobody ever mentions Rick quitting, and I wonder what he's told them. Whenever I go inside, Rick finds an excuse to keep himself occupied. I ask him to come have beers with me, to smoke a joint. He'd rather play on his computer, shooting monsters.

I'm eating toast one morning when he walks into the kitchen.

'Just so you know,' he says. 'We only use that bread for French toast.'

'Thanks,' I tell him.

We don't talk much after that.

★

The one person happy to have me back is Sorrel.

I become her new best friend. I watch her ride her bike and play checkers with her. She's only five but she can read and write and likes me to read her stories in the yard. Her favorite is this book about a vampire bunny that sucks the juice out of vegetables. I read that to her a dozen times, both of us laughing at the good parts like we've never heard them before. While she listens, she has a habit of twisting her hair in a knot around her forefinger, tight enough to turn her fingertip white.

When Clayton picks me up on Monday mornings, I always see her pale face peeking through the curtains, watching me go.

★

Apparently, we'd have a lot more work if it wasn't for the Indians. Just like the Chinese are responsible for all of Vancouver's problems, according to Clayton everything from bad weather to petty crime can be attributed to the local Native Americans.

'They're a bunch of gas-huffing retards.'

He goes on to tell me that the Natives are given a certain amount of tree planting contracts by law. Other companies are encouraged through tax breaks to support the Native community, because of its unemployment problem.

'So they get all our fucking cream just because their skin is red. If that's not racist I don't know what the fuck is.'

I should know better by this point, but I think I can change their opinion if I can only put it in their terms. 'Maybe they're getting something back for all the times we screwed them over.'

Clayton snorts.

'Chug-lover,' Brady says.

★

Campfires become our nightly ritual.

Clayton and his wife carry over the stereo from their trailer. If we're blitzed enough we make our own music. Walter brings a rusty harmonica that he blasts on. Annie has a five-string guitar and a voice like an old bullfrog. Everybody sings along.

'That's great,' Brady says, slapping his thigh. 'Listen to that, huh?'

We're always drunk, always stoned, always happy.

I'm flying, now – earning one-twenty, one-thirty a day. Then the ground gets gnarly. Rocky and rugged, you can feel every shovel stroke from your tailbone to your skull. We're paid a little more per tree but our totals have been cut in half.

'Don't worry,' Clayton assures us. 'We got some cream lined up for Monday.'

He's been hyping the cream all week, and I finally get the guts to ask him what he's talking about. He looks at me like I've got a dick growing out of my forehead. Cream is the holy grail of tree planting: soft, open ground that melts under your shovel like cheesecake. Usually, since it's so easy, the price per tree is dropped, sometimes to as little as a nickel. But Fred's hooked up a deal for us – ten cents a tree. Clayton slaps me on the back, tells me I'll plant my thousand.

'First rookie to hit a thousand always gets a case.'

I laugh. 'I'm the only rookie now that Rick's bailed.'

'Yeah,' Clayton scowls. 'But the dog-fucker wants in on this.'

We fall silent. Clayton picks up a rock, throws it skittering into the bush.

'Don't worry – I've told Fred what I think of that.'

I wonder if that was such a good idea.

*

The thought of that cream gets us through the rest of a gruelling week. Come Friday, we're ahead of schedule and Clayton takes the day off. The rest of us fuck around all morning and spend the afternoon smoking up, bragging about how sweet the cream's going to be. Brady tries to break a bottle on his head, doesn't, and almost knocks himself unconscious. Annie is surprisingly sympathetic. Maybe he's doing something right.

On the way back Walter tears up the dirt track, fishtailing Clayton's truck around every corner. We're singing, united, feeling like our motley crew has accomplished something. Then I see the caravan lumbering around the next bend.

'Shit!' I shout. 'Watch out!'

Walter's already seen. He pumps the brakes. The truck starts to swerve wildly. Walter's good – he holds the road – and I'm convinced we're going to squeeze past until the front wheels bite and jerk to the left. There's a crunch and the shriek of metal dragging across metal. Then we're sitting in silence and a cloud of dust.

One by one we pile out to assess the damage.

*

Clayton takes the news of our accident surprisingly well, considering we were wasted and mangled the front of his truck.

'Insurance will cover it,' he says.

But his face is hard. There's something else on his mind. We gather around. He looks out the window, clearing his throat.

'Just spoke to Fred.' He pauses, balls up a fist. 'He's decided to go ahead and plant the cream himself. Him, Neil, and Rick.'

The crew deflates. We slump around the mess table. I feel like the projector of my life has died just before the big finish. I bring my fist down on the table.

'That motherfucker.'

Clayton hands out beers. There's nothing else to say or do. We drink without enjoying it, smoke joint after joint like we're on a mission to get as fucked up as possible. After several hours, Annie and Brady walk back to our trailer, holding hands. Walter pukes and passes out on the table, telling Clayton over and over again how sorry he is about the truck. Clayton's wife is in bed. At the end it's just me and him. He stares moodily into his glass, harelip twitching in the way it does when he's wasted.

'You know,' he says suddenly. 'They offered to take you on. Fred and Rick. You can still plant the cream. I just didn't want to bring it up in front of the others.'

The strange part is, it's obvious he expects me to do it.

'Fuck that,' I say.

★

With the cream stolen, and no other contracts on the horizon, Clayton disbands the crew. Walter offers to drive Brady and Annie home in his car. Since Clayton has to go into town to see his insurance company, he says he can drop me off at the bus station. We all pile into our vehicles, realizing at the last minute that we won't see each other again. I roll down my window and they do the same. Walter waves.

'See you later, chug-lover!' Brady shouts.

Annie hits him, and he grins like a kid. I have time to flip him the finger and then we're heading off in different directions. When we pass Rick's place on the way into town, I ask Clayton to pull over. I've forgotten something. Fortunately, I don't have to deal with seeing the family. Sorrel's by herself in the front yard, reading. I walk over and sit down. She doesn't look up from her book.

'You're going, aren't you?'

'Yeah,' I say.

'Well, you might as well have this. I made it for you.'

She hands me a crayon drawing of a long-limbed stickman standing in a field of baby trees. He looks enormous, like a modern-day Paul Bunyan – except with a shovel instead of an axe. I smile, thank her, and give her a hug goodbye. Over her shoulder I can see a dark head peering through the living room window. I don't acknowledge it.

Sorrel walks with me to the truck, holding my hand. When I let go to hop inside she doesn't cry. She just stands at the end of the drive, growing smaller with distance.

★

At the bus station, Clayton and I shake hands. I don't know what to say.

'It's been an experience, man.'

'Sure,' he says, starting the truck. 'Take care in the city.'

I'm thinking about Clayton when I get off the bus in Vancouver. The air, even in the middle of downtown, tastes like sea – it's so rich and thick with salt. I stretch out in the park at Main and Terminal among the rest of the drug addicts that so terrify Clayton, and roll up the last of Annie's weed. But it's not the same – the buds have gone stale. I only smoke half the joint, flick the remainder into the grass. I should probably call my parents but don't think I'm ready for that, yet. Instead I just lay there, eyes closed, listening to the city sounds of traffic and screeching seagulls.

Sorry for Disturbing You

RICHARD KNIGHT

The first thing Ian noticed, as the stiff door lurched open in his hand, was the icy rain running in beads down the man's face. Now that it was all over, he was no longer sure if it had been rain or tears.

The man on the doorstep had looked directly into Ian's eyes. He seemed lost, hanging on to the doorframe for support. Drunk, Ian thought. Just my luck. The man straightened up and mumbled something.

'I'm sorry?'

'I used to know Edie and George Higham.' He swallowed hard, unable to continue his explanation. The names sounded familiar but Ian couldn't think why.

'Could I call a taxi? I don't feel very well.'

It was true he looked ill. Or very drunk. Ian heard the living room door click and looked round to see his daughter Corinne looking out.

'Who is it?'

'Go back in, Corry.' He looked at her knowingly, hoping not to frighten her, hoping she would go along with him. She peeped round the door.

The man looked at her and then at Ian.

'I'm sorry... I shouldn't disturb...' He faltered on the wet stone step and Ian's hand instinctively went out to hold him.

'I'm all right. I'm...'

'Come on. Come in for a moment.'

Corinne stepped back as Ian opened the door a little wider. The man watched his own feet deliberately climb the step, and placed a hand on the bright yellow painted wall inside the door, leaving a dark print. Ian guided him into the other room.

'Go and watch telly, Corry.' Corinne followed them into the room.

'I'm so sorry, I...'

'Sit down.' Ian pulled a wooden dining chair up. Not too comfortable. 'I'll call you a cab. Where do you live?'

The man brushed a hand through his grey, wet hair and looked at Ian, his eyes moist. He seemed not to have heard, or understood.

'Do you live locally?' Ian tried again, beginning to regret his decision to allow the stranger into his house. God knows what Karen would say when Corinne told her. Karen was staying at her mother's for a while. They had things to sort out.

The man fumbled in both inside pockets of his black jacket and finally retrieved a mobile phone, which shook in his hand as he turned it on.

'It's all right. I have a number here somewhere. What's this?' He stared hard at the small screen. 'Menu, directory, Bluebird taxis, call number.' He repeated each command as he pressed each button, placed the phone to his ear and looked at Ian.

'Sorry.' It was a whisper.

'Can I get you some water?'

'No, I'm... ' He lowered the phone and looked at it again. 'What have I done now? Menu, directory, Bluebird taxis, call number.' He pressed again, and looked up.

'Sorry,' he whispered again. 'It's ringing... hello, it's Michael, Michael Phelps. Yes, I need a taxi from 71 Hillside Road.'

Ian could hear the female voice ask where he was going to. Corinne pulled at his jumper.

'Who is he?' she mouthed. He shrugged.

'Go and watch telly, love.' This time she went.

As the man made arrangements with the taxi people, Ian rewound the last few minutes and came up with three questions. Who were Edie and George Higham? Why did the man knock when he had a phone anyway? And how did he know their house number? The man put his phone away. Ian could now smell the alcohol and another unspecific but foul odour.

'Ten minutes.' He smiled briefly. Ten minutes, Ian thought. What the hell am I supposed to talk about for ten minutes? He tried instinct.

'How do you know Edie and George?' The man breathed in hard and swallowed, his words forcing themselves up through his throat like a sobbing child.

'We were friends. Good friends. I liked George very much.' He looked around the room. 'It really has changed in here.' Of course. The previous owners. Ian remembered the name from the list of phone numbers on the kitchen wall. He'd spoken to George a few times after they'd moved in, about the unpredictable heating system. He'd been very helpful.

'It really has changed.' He said it again, shaking his head in disbelief, to fill the silence. Ian excused himself and went across the hall to the living room. Corrine was lying in front of the television, her head cradled in both hands. He came back.

'I'm sorry.' It was a whisper again, and he looked on the verge of crying. God, please, no, Ian thought. Another long silence.

'Are you sure you wouldn't like some water?' he asked.

'Of course I should be in hospital really.' The man ignored the question and blew his nose hard in a handkerchief.

'Are you ill?' It seemed obvious, but he needed to stop the silences. The man nodded, glassy-eyed, and looked at a space beyond Ian.

'Yes.' But no more information came. The smell was becoming more powerful.

'Should I call your doctor instead?'

The man shook his head slowly and looked down at his feet.

'They wouldn't come now. I'll be all right. I should really be in hospital you know.' There was another long silence. Ian drew back the curtain a little, hoping to see the beam of headlights outside the house but the street was deserted.

'So, it must have been a long time since you were here?'

'Twenty-two years.' The answer came immediately, like a times table answer.

'I should have been at the wedding but I wasn't allowed to go.' He looked at Ian, who noticed a tear run down the side of his nose. Or was it rain?

'I should've walked her down...' The knock at the door interrupted him. Ian answered the door, Corinne behind him. The taxi driver was already back at the gate. He waved. Thank God, Ian thought.

Back in the room, the man was rising unsteadily from the chair. Ian held his forearm gently and guided him out.

'Mind the step. It's a bit slippy.' The man seemed unsure how to negotiate the step and stood, staring at the dark bushes beyond the path. Then, with a sudden leap of faith, he took off without warning. There was little Ian could do to stop him falling in the mud, just in front of the bushes.

As he helped the surprisingly light man up, he saw the driver at the gate watching.

'He all right?' He sounded dubious about his passenger rather than concerned.

'I'm fine,' the man replied, putting out a leg to walk like a newborn foal.

'I'm sorry mate. I've had him before. You'll have to try someone else.' The driver turned and as the two of them swayed to maintain a precarious balance in the wind and rain, the car door slammed behind the bushes. Ian could see the rear lights moving slowly away through the leafless branches.

'Sorry.' The whisper was almost directly in Ian's ear. He turned and looked at the man, the cold rain smarting his eyes.

'You're OK. Come on. Let's try again.'

Back inside, Ian made a cup of tea in the kitchen and saw the number on the board. Edie and George Higham. He'd dialled the number before he realised what he was doing.

'George? It's Ian Harter. 71 Hillside? Hello. How are you?' They exchanged a few pleasantries.

'Having boiler trouble again?' George asked.

'Er no, actually. It's a... Well I'm not sure really. It's a problem... Do you know a Michael Phelps?' There was a long pause on the line, a silence full of some meaning Ian couldn't deduce.

'Yes. I do.'

'Well, he's here at the house. He's obviously not well. I don't like to send him home. He said he knows you.'

'Yes. Well, he did.' There was no further help, but Ian tried again.

'Do you think I should call his doctor or something? He doesn't seem well, kind of lost really. I'm not sure what to do.' Another pause. Ian could hear a female voice in the background.

'Look, I really don't know what to suggest.' George was apologetic, but firm in his determination not to help.

'Shall I put him on?' The idea came suddenly to Ian, in desperation.

'No. No.' The answer was quick and categorical. 'No, I don't think that's appropriate. Look, if he's bothering you I suggest you call the police. I'm sorry he's disturbing your evening but... I really must go. Sorry.'

'OK. Thanks for your...'

'Goodbye.' The line went dead, and Ian stared at the wall for a moment. The tea had stewed. From the living room he heard Corry laugh at something on the television.

Back in the other room, Michael had his eyes closed. Ian placed the tea gently on the table and his eyes opened.

'Sorry. Thank you. You're very kind.'

'Should I try another cab firm?' Ian asked, sipping his own tea. The man stared at the wall, where there was a black and white photograph of Karen with Corry on her knee, smiling. Ian thought of Karen at her mum's, and wished she were here now.

'I shouldn't be on my own really. I'll ring my social worker tomorrow. I'll be fine tonight. I have a neighbour who... It's the alcohol you see. I should have walked her down the aisle you know.' He looked imploringly at Ian, as though he might be able to help, to change something.

'Who?' The answer was another whisper that Ian couldn't understand.

'Sorry?'

'My daughter.' He nodded, as though Ian had successfully worked something out.

'They wouldn't let you?' He waited a long time.

'I'll ring again.' He began to feel for his phone again.

'No need. Look, I'll run you home. Just give me a few minutes.'

In the kitchen he called Karen and explained. She sounded tired, but not surprised.

'OK. Give me five minutes. Is she ready for bed yet?'

'No, not yet. I haven't had chance.' She laughed, which he liked. It was a kind of fondness. He felt better now she was coming.

Ian drained his mug and returned to the room, where Michael was staring at the photograph.

'Lovely family.' He smiled at Ian. 'Is your wife out?'

'She's on her way home. She'll be here soon, then I'll run you home.'

'Sorry.'

When Karen walked in the front door, she smiled at Ian and he raised his eyebrows and nodded towards the room.

'Mum!' Corry flung herself up at Karen and wrapped her legs round her back.

'Corry! My baby! How's my special girl?'

Ian introduced Karen to Michael. She helped Ian walk him to the car on the street outside, as Corry watched from the window.

'Sorry,' he whispered to Karen, and looked at her, his eyes full of tears or rain. She smiled and swept her long brown fringe behind her ear. The rain was still slicing through the cold night air.

'Don't be daft. You just take care, yeah? Ian will see you home. He'll make sure you're OK.' Ian looked at her standing in the rain. She smiled at them both, hugging herself in the cold, on the street, in the dark. He missed her being at home.

'You go in. It's cold.' She turned and trotted back up the path to Corry who was now in the doorway, framed by the light. Ian looked over his shoulder as Michael finally lunged in to the back seat, and saw Karen hugging their daughter, examining a dirty black mark on the wall.

On the way to his flat Michael apologised again.

'Don't worry. You make sure you ring someone if you still feel bad in an hour or two.' He paused whilst they turned a corner.

'Did you lose contact with Edie and George?' Ian wasn't hopeful of a reply and was surprised to get one.

'Yes. George was angry. Quite rightly. My wife too. She couldn't forgive me. We never speak now.'

Ian quickly knitted a story. An affair, a discovery, the separation, the alcoholism, the exclusion from his daughter's wedding. But the regret in this man's eyes could have told ten different stories. Ian didn't push for details. He could live without them, wasn't that curious.

91

Ian helped him inside the downstairs flat, which smelt of unwashed clothes and an acrid chemical smell he couldn't place.

'Sorry to disrupt your evening. You've been so kind.' Michael held his shaking hand out to Ian. His hand felt wet and cold, but he gripped hard, hanging on for a long time.

'Are you sure I can't ring anyone for you?'

'No, no. I'll be fine. You go home to your wife and daughter. Sorry.' His last word on the doorstep before the door closed with a soft click. Back in the car Ian waited a few minutes, with the engine running and the windscreen wipers beating time. He didn't know why, it just seemed best to wait, see if there was movement in the flat, let Karen have some time with Corry. After a while he saw Michael at the window drawing the curtains.

Back home Corry was in the bath. He could hear them chatting in the bathroom. He switched the television off, made two cups of tea and a glass of warm milk, and took the first careful steps up the stairs.

Mazzy at My Party

GUY RUSSELL

It sort of comes up by accident when I'm with John and Pete in the canteen, and they want to know who's coming.

'I mean, she may not,' I tell them. 'She sometimes did at my old house but only if she was in Europe. Even then, she has to work very hard. So, you know.'

Pete laughs.

'It's true,' I tell him. 'It's hard work. She can't always do what she wants to. Anyway, I'm going to get some really nice coffee for everyone, for later on.'

'She likes nice coffee, does she?' Pete looks like he's making a joke, or thinks he is.

'Yes,' I say. 'She likes Barcardi, too.'

'Really.'

'What's she like?' asks John. 'In real life?'

'Oh, the same as anyone else, really,' I tell him. I shrug. 'I mean, the important thing, if she comes, is just to treat her like a normal person.'

'Sure,' says John. He nods.

'Oh, sure,' says Pete.

On Saturday morning I go to Tescos and get some nice, good-value wine in and a few packs of Pils and some gin and mixers and some especially nice filter coffee. In my old house, my parties were famous for the really excellent coffee I'd make for the lategoers. I also get lots of bags of Twiglets and chipolatos and some cheese-and-onion flavour crisps.

Back home, I make a sangria in a big cauldron I borrowed off Janice, my neighbour, whom I've invited, obviously. I set out the wine and beer and lemonade in order on the kitchen table.

During the afternoon I tidy everywhere thoroughly and carefully move my collection of pottery houses upstairs. I dust and hoover so it looks shipshape for them all. Then I check again that the bathroom's quite spotless.

I'm just arranging the last cushions when the doorbell goes. It's John. He's got a bottle of wine in his hand, and a CD.

'Is er, Mazzy here yet?' he asks. He looks past me.

'No,' I tell him. 'You're the first.'

'I didn't want to miss her.'

He comes in and sits down on the settee. 'Is she definitely coming?'

'I don't really know,' I tell him. 'It'd have to be a last minute thing with her, you know. She's so –'

'But she might?' says John. He looks like a puppy expecting a treat. 'Oh – this is for you.' He gives me the CD he's brought. 'I made it myself,' he says. 'As a present.'

'That's really nice,' I say.

'It's got 'Dreamlover' on it,' he says, 'She won't mind, will she?'

'No of course not,' I say. 'That's great.'

'I just wondered, from what you said,' says John. 'It's just a tribute.'

'No,' I say, 'It's just, you know, gushy fandom she hates. It's like, she has to talk about herself all the time in interviews. When she's relaxing she wants to discuss other things, like fashion and travel and contemporary history.'

John nods fiercely.

Most people start arriving about eight. The ones who've got baby-sitters at home tend to be first. A few more might come a little bit later. Roger, Kevin and Betty from Pensions arrive quite early and we talk about computers and about Mike their boss.

After a while, Neil and Brian arrive with some cans of lager. Rog and Kevin go over to the hi-fi and take charge of what music to put on. Pete arrives. He says, 'Oh er, *Mazzy* hasn't come then?'

He laughs.

'No. Perhaps she can't make it,' I admit.

'Perhaps not,' says Pete. He laughs again.

Nigel from Systems Support arrives with his girlfriend, Jackie. Just behind them is Gill, Payroll Gill. She looks lovely. Some people apparently find her difficult to work with, but I've never found so.

'Hi Gill.' I give her an extra-daring smile.

'I made it, Colin,' she laughs.

'Someone said, er, Mariah Carey would be here,' says Jackie. 'Is that right?'

'Don't be stupid,' Nigel says to her.

'Someone told me,' Jackie says.

'I mentioned it to John,' I say. 'He's probably told everyone now.'

Jackie laughs. 'Oh, you are a one, Colin!' she says.

Gill has disappeared. I've just got Jackie a Malibu and a can of Carling for Nigel, when the doorbell goes again. I open up.

'Collykins, hi!'

Honestly, she's hardly changed at all. She's wearing a rather over-daring turquoisey minidress. She leans forward and kisses my cheek. 'Colly! Wow!'

'Hello Mazzy,' I say with pleasure. 'It's so nice you could come.'

'Fantastic! It's really fantastic being here tonight in your fantastic town, Collybabes,' she says. 'I've never been to

Leighton Buzzard before! It's fantastic! I really mean that. Uh, I hope,' she hesitates. 'Hope it's OK, Colly. I've brought a couple of friends.'

'Of course,' I beam. I don't mind, really. 'The more the merrier!'

'Oh great,' she says. 'This is Mick.' She turns to an older couple behind her. 'And this is –'

I think she says 'Ellen'. 'Hi!' I smile at them. 'Come in.'

'We met like, at Sketch and I told them about the party –'

'No, no problem,' I beam at them. 'Come in.'

I shake hands with Mick and smile at Ellen. Ellen is tall. Mick reminds me of someone. But they both seem very nice.

'Let me take your coats,' I say.

'Thanks, says Ellen.

'Cheers,' says Mick.

They go and sit down on the settee and immediately start snogging. They obviously won't be much trouble. Pete has come forward, looking strange. 'One time,' I introduce her to him, 'Mazzy brought her friend Arnold with her and – what happened, Mazzy?'

'Oh, Arnie!' laughs Mazzy. 'Always wild.'

'That's right. He ended up breaking one of my oldest pottery houses, one my mum had given me when I was little. A little boutique, actually.'

We laugh.

'Did you find it OK?' I ask, as I was in my old house in Ipswich the last time she came.

'No problem,' she smiles. 'Colin, baby, it's so great to see you. How is it?'

'Not bad,' I nod. 'New systems, you know. They're going to reallocate all our files onto a new DBMS. How's work with you?'

Mazzy sighs. 'Colin. Four months on the last album. And the book. And the tour. Sheez... But working with such a great bunch of people, yeah.' Thinking about this seems to cheer her up. 'My producer, he's a really great guy. He was great to work with. And my record company are fantastic. And everyone else I work with. But you know sometimes, Colin? Like, sometimes I wish I was just an office clerk like you. You know?'

'Sure,' I say sympathetically. 'Though we have problems sometimes too, you know.'

'Oh, Colin,' says Mazzy. I get her a large Bacardi and Coke. She won't have any chipolatos. She has to watch her weight.

The doorbell goes. It's Janice and Tony from next door.

'Hi,' they say.

'Hi,' I say. I take their coats from them. 'Tony, Janice, Mariah. Mariah, Tony, Janice,' I say. 'Jan's a hairdresser,' I say. 'Mariah's a singer.'

'Oh, what sort of thing do you sing?' I hear Janice ask, as I go into the kitchen to check on the sangria. John is out there drinking quite a bit of it. Brian and Neil are there too.

'The 1.8's got much better roadholding,' Neil is saying.

John grabs me. 'It *is* her!' he says.

'Who?' I say.

'Mariah!'

'Oh yes,' I say, 'I'll introduce you in a minute.'

'No, no, no,' says John. He looks terrified.

When I come back into the lounge, I notice Kevin is talking to Chas and Shona, who've just arrived. Pete has elbowed Tony and Janice away and is talking enthusiastically to Mazzy. He is leaning towards her closely. Well, I suppose she is the most beautiful woman in the room, apart from Gill from Payroll.

'I met Eric Clapton once,' Pete is saying, leaning forward. 'I was in the Tate Gallery, right, and he was in there with his bodyguard. I said to him, 'Hi, Eric.' And he said, 'Hi.''

'Awesome,' says Mazzy. She nods. 'Eric's a really great guy.'

'And I once knew somebody,' says Pete, 'Who knew Bono. In Ireland. Before he was famous, you know.'

'Bono's a really lovely guy,' Mazzy says, nodding.

The other Roger and his girlfriend and Betty and Alison play Dingbats for a while and then someone puts on the CD John brought and four or five people – there are about fourteen of us now at the party – dance about to it. John appears, and then crouches in the corner setting up my disco lights. When 'Dreamlover' comes on, I see him glance at Mazzy nervously but she doesn't seem worried. 'Dreamlover, Dreamlover,' my guests go, punching the air. Mazzy dances really well, but after a few songs she sits back down.

'I suppose for her it's like being at work,' Janice says to me.

It's nice that everyone seems to be integrating. I nearly didn't invite Mariah, I admit to Janice. But it seemed a shame not to just because of her not knowing anyone. And actually people are involving her in conversations in a really friendly way. Chas keeps telling her that he loved her last album, even though I'm sure he only listens to heavy rock.

I wonder where Gill is. I'm thinking I should go over and talk to Mick and Ellen, but they are still wrapped up in each other. Apparently Ellen is a dressmaker, which sounds interesting. Instead, I spend a while chatting to Nigel. He's going for a new job with Thames Water. Janice is now talking to Mazzy about hairstyling. 'Vidal's a really great guy,' Mazzy replies. I've finally managed to reach Gill, who's standing by the stairs, when Jackie comes over. 'They're having me on aren't they?' she says to me. 'That's not *really* Mariah Carey, is it?'

'Mariah Carey?' says Gill.

'Mariah Carey,' says Jackie. 'She's famous.'

'Don't be stupid,' says Nigel. He's just come down from the bathroom. 'She looks nothing like her.'

'No, it is actually,' I say. 'We were at school together, in Luton. Her dad worked for Vauxhall as well.'

'Oh, Mariah Carey,' says Gill. I smile at her.

'You do tell them, Colin, you old bastard,' says Nigel, slapping me on the back.

'That's incredible,' says Jackie, 'But you —'

'We're just friends. We've never gone out or anything,' I explain hurriedly. I glance at Gill. 'I mean, I had my 'O' levels to worry about. And she was very concerned about her career. Ballet lessons all weekend. That kind of thing.'

At that moment Mazzy comes out of the lounge and sees us by the stairs. Jackie turns and stares at her rather blatantly. Conversation stops. I start going red, but Mazzy has great social skills. She pays absolutely no attention and comes up and touches my arm.

'Colly, baby.'

'Maz,' I say.

'Colin, it's been a really fabulous party. Great. But it's tracks.'

'Tracks?'

'Making them, babekins.'

'Already?' I say in disappointment.

'I *know*,' she says, tilting her head. 'I'm really sorry, babe. Your Richard Judy — his TV show in the morning? He's a really lovely guy, they say — and I've got to do lunch with my British people — they're really fantastic — and I promised I'd meet Victoria for a workout?'

There's a gasp from behind me.

'And it's Wembley tomorrow?' She rolls her eyes. 'Oh Sheezus,' she says suddenly. 'I should have got you a BS pass!'

'No, no,' I say. 'I mean, it's not really my, you know —'

'Oh Sheez,' says Mazzy again. 'How could I have forgotten?'

'No really, Mazzy,' I say. 'It's just nice you're still taking your job seriously.'

Mazzy shrugs. 'It's the only way these days to stay at the top,' she says. 'Still, Collykins, it's been so great to see you again.'

'And you,' I say. I'm aware of several people listening to us talk. Mick and Ellen have come to stand behind her. Great-Uncle Bill...! That's who Mick reminds me of.

'Great to meet you, Mick, er, Ellen,' I say. I feel bad that no one really made the effort to speak to them. They're probably quite interesting, even if they are gatecrashers. But they seem happy enough together.

I open the door. Mazzy's car is taking up most of the cul-de-sac. I hope the Wilsons over the road are back from line-dancing.

'Sheez, I said to the driver to park down the street,' complains Mazzy. 'I know how you hate embarrassment.' She kisses me on the cheek.

'Mazzy, you're so thoughtful.'

We step out onto the pavement.

'Bye,' we say, 'Bye. Bye.'

'Have a good er, gig,' I call.

I go back inside. Everyone's grouped together and it's noisy, then it goes quiet, and then noisy again.

'It *was*,' shouts Nigel. 'Colin, why didn't you say?'

'Sorry?' I say.

'Mariah!'

'Oh, Mazzy hates fuss,' I explain. 'She's a very ordinary person, basically –'

'It was such a fantastic party,' says Janice.

'It's been a totally incredible party,' says Jackie.

'Mariah and I were just talking about meeting Bono and that,' says Pete.

'Fancy you knowing her, Colin,' says Shona, coming up close to me. 'And never telling us! You're so *modest* –'

Betty puts an arm round me. 'You are a deep one, Colin.'

'Colin's great,' says Alison from Admin, who's virtually ignored me all year.

They all stare at me as if I'm really interesting.

'I don't think she's all that good, actually,' says Gill.

There's a silence.

I smile at her.

'She's gone?' says John, looking round anxiously. He's just come out of the kitchen with Neil and Brian.

'With those old ones, there's no synchromesh on the first gear,' Brian's saying to Neil.

'I thought she was lovely,' says Janice.

'Mariah's a really lovely girl,' says Pete mistily. 'She's special, isn't she? I mean the way she likes being with ordinary people who treat her in an ordinary way. I think some stars really do. It's the way they stay in touch, you know.'

'It's been a fantastic party,' says Jackie.

'I find they start going underneath the sills,' Neil is saying.

'I must say, she always stood out when she was younger,' I say. 'You could tell she was talented even then. She'd even sing the answer to her name at register.'

'I never realised she'd lived in England,' says Shona. 'In Luton. It's not very glamorous.'

'They make up those official biographies, you know,' says Nigel, nodding, 'to fit in with people's fantasies of them.'

'It's public relations,' adds Pete knowledgeably.

I look at Gill and think about that really nice coffee I bought. I smile at her. 'Could you give me a hand?' I ask brazenly. In the kitchen, she puts the cups out.

'Have you been having a nice time?' I ask.

'Oh er, yes,' she says, but she refuses a cup and saucer for herself, sounding weary. 'I won't have one, I've got to be off.'

'It's really nice coffee, I got it –'

Her mouth hardens. 'I'm really really tired.'

There's a pause.

'You could, er, erm,' I feel myself going red, 'If you, tomorrow –'

'I'm busy tomorrow,' she says. 'Although obviously I'm not meeting "Victoria". Unlike Mazzy.'

Gill sounds weird. I'm not following her train of thought, so I don't know what to say.

When I look up from filling the cafetière, Gill is on her way out. Janice and Jackie are blocking the doorway.

'D'you think she could get *me* a backstage pass, Colin, even if *you* don't want one?' asks Janice.

'And me?' says Jackie.

'And me?' says John behind them.

'You could get her to give you several, and pass them on,' says Shona.

I'm pushed backwards. My guests jostle me by the sink and keep saying 'Mariah.' No one mentions the coffee. They keep asking me for daft details about Mazzy at school. Alison wants me to go to Wembley or somewhere with her, and it's hard work putting her off. Pete and Nigel start having an argument about which of Mazzy's albums is the best. Jackie tells Nigel she likes her more than he does. Then John puts 'Dreamlover' on again, and everyone runs into the lounge and starts going funny over it.

I'm left with Brian and Neil, who've just reached a conversational pause.

'Here Colin,' goes Brian. 'This coffee, it's really nice.'

'Yes, it is, isn't it?' I say. And, as he's interested, I start telling him where I got it.

Blue + Yellow

CHRIS KILLEN

There is another girl, too – his girlfriend – away on a placement year in the States. He speaks to her sometimes, quietly, from the other room. Amelia. She also paints. Clair doesn't know much more than this because she doesn't want to ask. When the phone rings late at night it's her. When it rings, and she looks at the clock, then it's her, it's her, it's always her.

He goes through to the back. He answers. Clair's on his bed. All she can hear is the low warm hum of his voice. Sometimes they'll talk for an hour. She arranges her limbs carefully beneath the covers. Framed in the dress mirror, her eyes are dark holes in the porcelain moon of her face. She sees herself done in thick oils: a violent white swirl pricked twice with black – dot-dot – and a bitten red dash for the mouth.

On the walls are paintings. A view from the window. A white chair, propped against a desk. She looks at it enviously. She places herself in it, with her hair more curling than it is, and with sunlight caught in the black. Her shoulders curve in fine, glistening points.

I love her too, you know, he told her.

I know, said Clair, as casually as she could. She understood the situation; she knew what she was getting into. It's not like we're gonna get married or anything, she'd said.

And then she forgot about it, pushed it beneath the surface. Only every day it comes up like a buoy.

Clair's half asleep when he finishes. He stands at the foot of the bed looking; she can feel him there. He pushes off his jeans, crawls under the covers, and leans over her, kissing her neck as she curls like a rabbit towards the wall.

Hey, he whispers. You still awake? He kisses her neck, her hair catching in his stubble as he pulls away to get comfortable.

Who was that calling? she wants to ask. She wants to hear him say the name. It's already ringing in her head, anyway: Amelia Amelia Amelia. He might as well say it.

He drapes his arm across her waist, shuffles up behind her, and she can feel his dick touch her buttock. It's hard. She loves him. She keeps her eyes closed and pretends she's asleep. Then she is.

Drinks with her ex-university friends, Kate and Simon.

George is painting me.

Really? They don't know what else to say.

In the toilets she goes on to Kate about Amelia, over and over. He was on the phone for an hour. I don't know what to do. It should just be me.

Simon hears the other stuff. George has some work accepted for an exhibition. George sold another one last week.

How's the writing, they ask, but she doesn't listen. They're inching away from her, turning themselves into acquaintances across the table. They are bored.

George is painting me, she says.

How can you love two people, she thinks at work, drawing cubes on the till receipt. How can love divide itself? She thinks of it as something uncontainable, something that can't be sectioned off. His love for her, and his love for *her* – how can they differ? She thinks of oil paints in thick broken tubes.

If his love for her is blue and his love for Amelia is yellow, then there is just green.

I can't change him. This she knows. All I can be is myself, and if I'm not enough, then I'm not enough. I can't ask. I knew what I was letting myself in for.

The lights are bright and cold above. There is dust on the shelves. An old man puts a tray of watercolours and a brush down slowly on the counter.

Without him, there's just this.

In his studio, she creeps up to the easel. He's out, buying things for dinner. Only a hand and wrist so far. He's washed the background a pale olive. She looks at her own hand, turns it in the light, bends her fingers into the same position. Her skin is paler, very slightly paler. The paint hand has a freckle on it, just above the index. Its nails are bitten.

Clair goes over to his oils. She wonders what he'd say if he caught her unscrewing the cap off the black. It's caked on. She has to hold it between her knees and when she gets the top open it's left marks on her jeans. She dabs her finger in and carefully places the dot in the same place: just above her left index.

She's changed into her work skirt by the time he returns. He doesn't seem to notice. The kettle's on. Pasta and red wine, for my beautiful girl. She presses herself against him, enjoying making it awkward for him to stir. She bites his ear and he laughs and pushes her away.

After dinner they sit on the sofa.

Stop that, he says, pulling her fingers from her mouth, a nail caught between her teeth.

Amelia called again. I don't know what to do. It's eating me up.

What? What's up? Kate has just answered the phone. She was going to sleep.

I feel sick. I know, I know. I shouldn't go on about it,

but I don't know what to do. I can't bear to think what'll happen in September.

We've been over this. I don't know what else you want me to say.

I'm afraid to ask him what's going to happen. I don't think I'm changing a thing...

I was sleeping. It's late.

She calls every other day.

Kate hangs up on her.

Now there are two hands, two arms, a body, and a neck. Everything except the head. Clair's been watching it grow, gradually, and arranging herself next to it whenever she gets the chance – whenever he goes out.

I'm thinner in the painting. My breasts are very slightly bigger. The nipples are dark. If only there was a mirror in the studio.

In his bedroom, while he's washing, she stands in front of the long dress mirror and pulls off her sleeping shirt. She pinches her nipples again and again until they darken and smart.

Do you have any photos of her, she asks once they're in bed.

Of who, he mumbles, almost asleep.

She can't say the name out loud. She tries but she can't. She thinks she saw one once, in one of his drawers. The girl had blonde hair and a tan. It's hard to remember. She only saw it for a second, as he was getting out a key.

His breathing deepens. It comes in slow, broken brushes against her neck.

Come over, he says. I want to show you something.

He's smiling as he opens the door. He is wearing a shirt – not a painting shirt, a smart black one – and clean-shaven.

He takes her through to the studio. She remembers a time at school, when she was told in advance about an award they were giving her. It was supposed to be a surprise but someone let it slip, so she had to stand up in front of a hall full of people and feign shock and happiness.

I've finished it, he says as she walks round to look. What do you think?

It is a painting of a girl, framed in green. The girl has dark blue eyes and light brown hair.

Clair?

She's crying.

What is it?

Fucker.

What?

You heard me.

She sits on the floor and sobs into her knees. He crouches down, and puts his arm awkwardly across her shoulders. Did you think… did you think it was you? He's whispering. She doesn't answer. I'll do one of you next. I'm sorry. I'll paint you next. You should have said. Silly. He brushes the hair out of her face, tries to kiss her on the ear but she pulls away.

Later she's calmed down. He cooks. They go to bed with the food still sitting on their stomachs. It's so early he's had to draw the curtains against the blue. I'm sorry, he whispers again. The wall has a postcard tacked to it: a painting of a window with the curtains drawn. She stares at it and doesn't answer.

Just after one they both wake. The phone is ringing in the back. Stay here, she wants to say. Don't answer. He gets up, and she watches him walk through in his boxers, she hears him speaking.

A digital alarm clock sits on the table next to the bed. He talks from 1:06 to 2:14. Hearing him come back, she turns to the wall and draws her knees to her chest, arranging herself asleep. You awake? he whispers once he's climbed in behind her. Yes, she says after a pause. She needs to talk to someone. She needs to be hugged. So she turns and puts her arms around him and holds him as tight as she can.

Obscured by Clouds

ADAM CONNORS

Of all the rooms in the Abbey, the Archive Room is our most sacred. It's a cramped, dry space accessible only from the basement on the east side of the building, and except for the gradual accretion of the wax cylinders which line the walls on all sides, it has remained untouched since the plates were first discovered here, many generations before I was born. I was meditating on the track we call 'Shine', taking a copy onto a wax cylinder so I could review it later, when I heard Durga's footsteps moving softly across the floorboards above my head.

I paused in the lull that comes between tracks and waited for him to arrive. Durga was a pale, fragile boy, still marooned in the uncertainties of puberty. He stood awkwardly in the doorway, his eyes unnaturally large in the dim light, his face stark with emotion.

'Excuse me, Brother Roger,' he said. 'Father Michael is calling for you.'

'Very well,' I replied.

I turned back to the phonograph, reluctant to leave. Father Michael was our Abbot, and it was he who took me in when I first came to the Abbey nearly forty years ago. He was like a father to me, but now he was dying, and as his most senior initiate it was my duty to select his Funeral Track.

'Come inside a moment,' I said. 'Perhaps there is time

for one more plate before we go.'

Durga nodded and closed the door behind him. He crouched on the rail next to me, his body tightening when he saw that I was working directly from a black plate. All the initiates have their own phonograph capable of playing the wax cylinders, but the plates themselves are accessible only to the senior monks and are never allowed to leave the Archive Room.

I bent more closely to the phonograph and began winding the delicate mechanism, cocooned in the buttery light from the candle as the room filled with the urgent, aching music of the Sound Archive.

The plates, in case you haven't been fortunate enough to see one for yourself, are slightly less than two hand-spans across, and etched with an exquisite filigree of concentric circles so fine that their surfaces shimmer when they catch the light. We know it's the etchings that hold the sound, but the means to create the plates themselves is beyond us now. They come to us from before the Fall, and they tell the story of the last days. A final message from the ancients, and a warning of the cycle that lies before us. I refer to the black plates, of course. The silver plates also reside in the Archive, but they yield nothing to the bone needles that we use in our phonographs.

Much of what is contained in them is strange to us, referring as it does to events that took place before the Fall. But we meditate on their music so that we might learn from the wisdom of the ancients. We know little of that time, only that the people once possessed a great power, and that when that power dwindled it signalled the end of their cycle and the beginning of our own.

Listening to those strange sounds in the warm, enclosed space of the Archive Room, it's easy to imagine what it must have been like back then. When the power was beginning to fail, and the people knew that their end was coming fast. The giant engraving machines running day and night, belching noxious fumes as they etched the last of the black plates. What a humble and selfless people they must have been, who used the last dregs of their fading power to leave this gift for us. Their words are a call to arms, a desperate plea to the seers, the painters, and the pipers, from a dying people. That we might one day come to understand the full value of their legacy.

The music faded around us, and we were lost for a moment in the visions that accompany it. Suddenly, Durga turned to me with renewed urgency.

'Brother Roger,' he said. 'We must go.'

He went to stand, but I ignored him. 'There was one other I wanted to play for you,' I replied.

Durga hesitated. 'But Father Michael?'

'Not yet,' I insisted. I was not ready to see Father Michael just yet.

Durga watched attentively as I unclipped the casing to reveal the delicate system of fly-weights and drive belts that turn the central disk, working deftly and with the benefit of many years of familiarity to clean them ready for the next plate. As I lifted the plate from the Archive Box, its beautiful surface caught a stray shaft of sun from the vent above our heads, and I paused for a moment to admire the glittering sparks of light that played across its surface, reflecting on the rich palimpsest of secrets locked inside. Durga saw it too. He moved as if to touch the plate and I recoiled instinctively from him.

'My apologies, Brother Roger,' he said, retracting his hand hastily.

I lowered my head by way of apology, turning away to slot the plate onto the phonograph. I had not intended to snub Durga. The plates are incredibly fragile and I am naturally protective of them. For us, our reverence for the Archive is amplified by that sense of continuing fragility. But the fear that one day it might vanish altogether, that we bear witness only to the receding echo of something that is already lost, is something that permeates the lives of everyone in the Abbey. We seek to preserve the Archive as best we can, even though we know that it is by nature a transient and fading thing. This is why we have come to rely so heavily on the wax cylinders in recent years. We channel the music from the plate into a second needle, which etches the sound back into the surface of a wax cylinder. Of course, the wax cylinders are far more fragile than the plates, but in return we get maybe twenty or thirty services from each cylinder before it deteriorates beyond value.

As soon as the first notes of the next track began to fill the enclosed room, Durga turned to me sharply.

'My mother's Funeral Track?' he commented.

'Mine too,' I replied.

★

Durga came to the Abbey the same way all the boys come to the Abbey, the same way I came to the Abbey over forty years ago. In a moment of unquestioning epiphany.

It had been a little over a month since I'd been called to the settlement to give Last Rites to Durga's mother. It was an unusually clear morning, and as I'd left the Abbey a line of golden sunlight had flooded eagerly into the valley ahead of me. My Brothers were going about their business in the grounds, some working in the small field next to the Abbey, others tending to the hives that produce the wax for our cylinders. The late summer air was crisp but readily warmed by the sun, and the ground was moist against my sandalled feet. I pulled my robes closer to me, and began the short descent into the settlement.

No matter how many times I visit the settlement, I am always taken back by the hardship of life there. The people live or die on what little they can grow in the hard, grey soil around them. There is no time or energy to set aside anything as security against a bad harvest. It is a short, hardworking life in which starvation and disease are rife. We are insulated from this somewhat within the Abbey, since our food-stocks are strengthened by donations from the settlement in return for our services to them. It is a difficult thing, to think that we accept donations from such a hard put upon people. But we never ask them for anything, and most interestingly, the years that see the worst harvests and the hardest conditions, are also the years in which the people give most to the Abbey.

Durga had seen me appear at the top of the street and he came running out to greet me. He was a clumsy child, slapping through the muddied streets towards me, heedless to the privation and filth around him. He took my arm and hurried me towards his family's hut.

Inside, it was unnaturally quiet. The air was thick with the combined smells of firewood and dampness and cooked meat, all pressed into that tight space alongside the heavy, syrupy stench of death. The fire flickered weakly in the corner, clearly stoked in the morning to chase away the dawn mist, but now succumbing to the pervading dampness itself. Maggie Farrow lay on a roll-mat in the far corner, her husband and their surviving children clustered tightly around her. Martin, Durga's father, turned to me and bowed respectfully.

'I'm sorry to be a trouble, sir,' he said. 'I don't think she can last much longer.'

I nodded, and followed Martin as he gently shooed away his children. I squeezed past them, their dark eyes watching me sullenly, and knelt next to Maggie. Her face glowed with a sallow, waxy sheen in the dim light. Needles of pure white picked out the sweat that coated her broad cheeks, and her grey eyes stared at the ceiling, fixed and unblinking. I leant in close, smelling suddenly her stale odour, and began to recite the words taken from the Sound Archive that we call the Last Rites. The words tell the story of the last days of the ancients, the end of the world as they knew it, and we speak them whenever somebody is close to death. A plaintive cry, the litany of disasters that befell the ancients, crumbling into delirium. The death throes of a lost people. After years of reciting these words they rise naturally to my lips, spilling out in a tight, low utterance, an insistent, nagging rhythm that transcends the words themselves. Building to the final challenge and response that signifies the ultimate decisive act that heralded the ancients' acceptance of their fate. The words that gave birth to the Sound Archive. The last words that anyone in the settlement hears.

I lifted Maggie's head gently with my hand.

'Right?' I asked.

'Right,' she agreed.

Her voice was cracked and breathy but filled with certainty. She nodded painfully. Then her head fell back, and her eyes closed. I glanced up and saw that Martin and his children had gathered around me. I knew what was expected next, selecting the Funeral Track is one of the most important services we offer the settlement. I regarded Maggie's blunted features. Her skin was pale and papery, but despite the ravages of illness it was clear that she had been an attractive woman. She had an open, unquestioning appearance, and I sensed her strength as a solid presence in the family. Only the Funeral Track can bring meaning to such senseless loss. The brief, fierce lives endured by the people of the settlement.

'Breathe,' I said, turning to meet Martin's look.

'Breathe?'

He looked nonplussed for a moment. He glanced uncertainly to his children. I hummed the first few seconds of the track. A heavy, languid sound that builds into an ecstasy of violent, thrashing emotion. Suddenly Martin's face shattered with recognition, and for the first time tears streamed freely down his cheeks.

'Such a beautiful track,' he whispered, kneeling and taking Maggie's hands in his own. 'Such a beautiful track...' He looked up suddenly. 'Thank you, Brother Roger... Thank you.'

114

We stayed like that for a while. Martin whispering tearfully to his wife, and me standing uncertainly over him. After some time, I stepped quietly away and headed for the door. Martin stopped me before I could leave, pressing the usual fee into my hand. 'Thank you.'

That night, we wrapped Maggie's body in the traditional way and carried it back up to the Abbey for the Funeral Service. We stood together in the Great Hall. Myself at the front, my face lifted towards the vaulted ceiling, the Farrow family clustered in the centre of the room, rain-soaked and pitiful. The wrapped body of Maggie Farrow was laid out before them, equally rain-soaked and muddied on one side. The rest of the settlement clustered silently behind. I gave the signal, and the hall filled suddenly with the music of the Funeral Track. Around the balustrade, five or six of my brothers knelt over their phonographs, their faces locked in concentration as they fought to stay in time with each other. The membranous funnels of the phonographs pointed upwards so that the sound could climb to the very top of the high ceiling before crashing down on us. That feeling. I felt it for the first time on the day I attended my own mother's funeral, and it has never left me since. That overwhelming sense of certainty. Of comfort and relief that only the Sound Archive can bring. I watched as the music played out, Martin sobbing freely, his children clustered tightly around him, staring up at the ceiling in bewilderment.

When the track had finished, my brothers took Maggie's body. They would bury her in the fields that surround the Abbey, such that her remains would bring new life to the soil.

Martin Farrow nodded gratefully, his body shaking with his sobs. Standing at the head of the great hall, my hands clasped in front of me, I felt that I cast a noble, comforting figure. Martin's two eldest daughters helped him and his youngest daughter as they left, but Durga remained behind. He waited uncertainly for a moment, and I stood patiently for him. He knew nothing, only that he had been moved by the music, that he longed to remain close to it. At last, he worked up the courage to step forward and approach me.

'Please, Brother Roger...' he said. His voice was rough, disjointed English straight from the fields, but it shook with passion. 'Please,' he said again. 'I want to stay.'

★

Sitting beside me now in the cramped Archive Room, his eyes, like mine, were heavy with tears.

'Come,' I said resignedly. 'Let's not waste any more time.'

We locked the door of the Archive Room behind us and walked together up the narrow staircase that leads back to the Great Hall. The ground floor of the Abbey was deserted and the Great Hall ominously silent. We hurried up the sweeping staircase that leads to the balustrade, and from there into the living quarters where Father Michael waited.

The hallway outside his room was crammed with our brothers waiting for news of his condition. Their anxious whispered discussions and muted shufflings filled the tight space with a fraught and oppressive miasma. They fell silent when they saw us, acknowledging us with deferential nods and pressing themselves against the wall so that we could pass.

When I knocked, Father Michael called through the door, and I entered alone to find him hunched over his phonograph. He smiled when he saw me, straightening his head with great effort. Seeing him like that, I was shocked by how old he had begun to look. He was once a strong and powerful man, but his recent illness had stripped him of his former power and left him timid and sunken. He clasped his hands lightly in his lap, his knees pressed together. He paused for a moment, his eyes gazing distractedly ahead of him.

'Father Michael?' I said. 'I'm sorry if I disturb you.'

Father Michael smiled vaguely. 'It's good to see you, Brother Roger,' he said.

'Thank you, Father,' I replied. 'How are you feeling?'

'Comfortably numb, Roger,' he sighed. 'Comfortably numb.'

He stood, very slowly, levering himself up with his hands against his knees, and shuffled to the window. Standing, he looked more crumbled than ever.

'Father? Is it time?' I asked.

He smiled tiredly. 'Almost, old friend... But there is something I must tell you first.'

He glanced over his shoulder and gestured for me to come closer.

'Come to the window for a moment,' he said.

I closed the door behind me and stood next to him at the window. Outside, the far side of the valley rose sharply in front of us, the last glow from the setting sun lightening the sky in a ragged line along the top of the ridge. A few fires burned in the settlement below, but otherwise everything was utterly dark.

'What do you see?' he asked.

'Nothing, Father,' I replied. 'Darkness.'

'Indeed.'

There was a pause, and then Father Michael said:

'Men are such fractious creatures, Roger. Ever since the Fall we have been dispersing, fading into the landscape.' Tears streamed from his eyes and formed rivers in the lines around his mouth that shone in the lamp-light. 'We are dying, Roger. We are all dying. *In the midst of life...* the plates warn us. *Here today, gone tomorrow.* And when the Archive is gone we will be left to grub around in the dirt like cattle.' He gripped my arm sharply. 'Roger, I have a plan. Something that can preserve our way of life, if only you will do as I ask.'

'Anything, Father,' I replied.

'A pilgrimage. You must take the Archive to the other settlements and share it with them so that they might know it. Do you see? All this time we have sat quietly here and watched the Archive dwindle...'

'But we can't –'

'Think of it... All those settlements out there in the darkness, more numerous than the stars. All those souls who know nothing of the Sound Archive. Who have never received the Last Rites, or heard a Funeral Track. All those people, Roger, like the stars themselves... Utterly desolate.'

I stared hard out into the blackness, imagining them out there. The poor lost people huddled together. Valley after valley, waiting for the Sound Archive to bring them light. My mind worked furiously. It would be a simple matter to construct a phonograph that could be carried in a pack or transported by mule. A few modifications might be necessary to make it more robust, more readily repairable. I would have to take spare needles with me, spare fly-weights and drive belts, but that was a simple matter. I tried to imagine which plates we would select for such a momentous journey. How we could ensure that they came to no harm.

'I would have to build a padded chest of some kind,' I said. 'For the plates.'

'Yes. And then you must send the people back here to us. You must persuade them to join us, to unite with us under the Archive. It's the only way.'

He turned away from the window with an air of finality, as if the outside world no longer held any interest for him now that his legacy had been passed on. He started back towards his desk, but before he got there an attack of dizziness overcame him and he slumped heavily onto his bed. His face sagged. The fire had deserted him again. It broke my heart to see him like that, but at the same time a newfound joy rose inside me. How long we had selfishly kept the Archive to ourselves. How foolishly we had hoarded it and refused to share it with the other settlements.

'And... And what of my Funeral Track?' Father Michael asked, timidly.

'Shine,' I replied, confident now in my choice.

He smiled, his eyes sharp with emotion.

'A very beautiful track, Roger... Very beautiful.'

I helped him to lie flat, his lips moving softly as he recited the track to himself. He lay there for a moment, his breathing laboured, before his eyes eased shut and he slipped into a fitful sleep.

Outside, in the hallway, there was a rustle of muted whispering.

'Brother Roger?' Brother David asked. 'What news?'

'Shine,' I replied.

There was a general murmur of approval.

'A wise choice,' Brother David said, grasping my forearm reassuringly. 'And now you will read the Last Rites?'

I shook my head. 'Soon,' I said. 'But first I have something to tell you all... A great undertaking Father Michael has bestowed on us.'

My brothers crowded close as I told them of our pilgrimage. How Durga and I would set out from the Abbey to share the music of the Sound Archive. Durga learning from me as we travelled from settlement to settlement, and both of us teaching the wisdom of the Sound Archive to those we met. I described to them how we would play for the elders of each settlement and invite them to join us. How gloriously they would greet us, the people pouring from the fields to honour us. And how gratefully they would receive us, that we would come to deliver them. The lines of pilgrims who would be inspired to make their own journeys, travelling back to the Abbey to make their offerings.

'Brother Roger,' Durga interrupted, nervous in this enclosed space amongst so many senior monks. 'What if they don't listen? The other settlements, what if they don't care about the Archive? If they have something in its place?'

The other monks turned to me suddenly, their faces etched with fear, desperate for me to reassure them. I reflected for a moment on their troubled eyes, filled with such uncertainty. Men are such lonely creatures, I thought. So desperate for any form of consolation. Then I laughed suddenly, not meaning to hurt Durga's feelings but buoyed up by my own enthusiasm.

'Oh, but they must,' I replied. 'They simply must.'

Relief rippled through the hallway, and the other monks surged forward as one to congratulate us. To touch us, to be near us. Because in that moment all of our doubts fell away, and we became a new people, right there, united in this glorious and sacred duty. To become vessels of the ancients and share the Archive with those poor lost savages out in the darkness. To deliver the settlements from their ignorance. And to never tolerate darkness again.

The Sanctuary

JACQUELINE MCCARRICK

She wanted to go into the bedroom but was afraid. She knew what she would do if she could not find him (and of course she would not find him): clamber into the bed, burrow under the thick white duvet and the Foxford throw, there since winter, when they had left, when the pain had so tellingly returned. She would turn on her side, clutch at his side of the sheets, at his pillow, attempt to pull something of his life back. Maybe she'd find a hair or a feather or a fragment of skin, something. But she would not go in just yet; she did not want to know, for certain, that he was not inside, sleeping, or reading his book with the lamp on.

She straightened the six Paolozzis in the hall. She was aided by the small pencil marks he had drawn on the wall around the corners of the brushed-chrome frames. His eye was always so precise, a spirit level. She looked up at the sun-filled skylight he'd built to frame the North Star: dust-motes swirled in the long rays. She went into the living room and pulled up the coffee-coloured blinds. He had wanted to redesign the windows so that the glass met in a geometric point; a jetty out to the sanctuary during the day, and to vast black skies and the stars at night. He had wanted to schedule the work for May. She expected it would have been finished by now.

It was as if they'd just left. A black leather glove lay palm down on the coffee-table. She picked it up and put her hand inside half expecting to find his. There was a sense that the house had been waiting for them to return. For they could just as well have been gone for the afternoon; gone for a stroll down Cotter's Lane to her father's like they had done in October. They'd picked blackberries along the Lane then, eaten them as they walked. Even at the time, she remembered, she had not wanted to be here in this borderland wilderness, where, she considered, a life could pass without making a mark, become slight and pathetic like the tiny silver moths that came out at dusk and were dead by morning. She wanted to be in the flat in London, helping him with the Practice, shopping in Marylebone on a Saturday (there was meaning for her in that life), and she simply could not understand his love of this place. It was not picturesque like Kerry, nor fabulous and strange like Connemara. It appealed to him, she decided, partly because it was unlikely. He always saw what others could not, what was hidden in a thing, its numinous potential. Living in this house had softened him, and she had watched his once uncompromising modernism give in, ever so slightly, to the pastoral.

In the sanctuary a hare squatted tensely behind a rock. She knew it was a hare by its legs and ears and long hay-brown body. (They had come to know the different species of birds, rodents, plants and flowers; had become alert to bird cries.) The hare halted, watching something intently beyond the rock, and she was reminded of him. Ever since the service she'd noticed how certain things, for no particular reason, brought him to her mind. The pink and red pansies in the flowerbed outside Kensal Green crematorium; the grey-haired stranger's face on the Edgware Road; words in books and newspapers her eye would randomly fall upon. ('A characteristic of grieving,' somebody had called it, this revelation in quotidian things; far from bringing her comfort, she found the experience disturbing.) Now, it seemed, even the sanctuary reflected him, as if he, with his magnanimous life force, had returned to nature and was down there influencing its flow, whipping up arcane schemes and intrigues like Prospero.

The hare moved on for reasons known only to it, under the hedge into the precariousness of Ramsey's field. She wanted to warn it, to tap the window: *don't go in there, you'll get yourself killed.*

She went into the kitchen. All those jars of vitamin pills and miracle-cures: dried seaweeds and mushrooms, B17 (a banned vitamin she'd had to buy on the black market), sealed packs of bark from some obscure tree. Cupboards of pills, rows of cancer cookbooks. All that hope and promise of hope: over, over, over. She plunged the books into a black rubbish bag, then gathered the glass jars of beans and pulses – anything that could still be eaten – onto the island. He had built it in November: a solid pine work-board atop grille-fronted beech cupboards. Driven, when he shouldn't have, to B&Q in Newry for the materials and built it himself; a place for her to prepare his coffee enemas, his organic juices, his vitamin cocktails. November. That's when the pain had come back. That awful pain that she could not truthfully imagine having in her own body. For someone in such a fragile remission, he had done far too much.

She checked the sell-by dates. Dad might be able to use some of these, she thought, then packed the jars of rice and pulses into the green cloth Superquin bags.

He'd come to love her father, had been responsible for her and her father's truce. (The move here had brought them into daily contact with him, a familiarity that, over time, had caused her to forget, a little, her father's faults; in particular, his drinking.) The old man had been quiet lately up in the house; on his best behaviour. She had decided to stay there with him rather than here, as she didn't want to be alone.

Eventually she must go into the bedroom: she needed clothes. When they had left in January, she had not wanted to make a fuss about how long they'd be gone; they'd flown to London with two suitcases, one each, containing no light clothes. But his pain was such, she thought, that he must have known the trip would be for longer. And if so, what was he thinking as he left this house – did he sense he would not be back? Had he come here to die, she wondered? Had that been the point of it all, the hurried relocation, the mad search for a rural idyll? Perhaps he did have such a presentiment; their conversations in the last year had been oddly elliptical, and she had not probed his fears should such talk spoil their fight, for it was always *their* fight. And so she insisted they take little: a few warm clothes, shoes. That way he would be bolstered into thinking: *this new pain is a small thing, a glitch, and look, she is not preparing for the worst, she believes in me and my ability to conquer this, and soon we will be home.* She hoped it had gone something like that.

She went into the utility room and opened the door to the back garden. The high grass almost obscured the garden furniture on the concrete steps. All the plants were overgrown and dry. Some had died. She'd have to get the gardens seen to before the estate agent came to view the house; maybe her father would do it if he'd time.

As she walked down the steps she noticed, on the ground, and wrapping around the corner of the house, a trail of yellow rose-petals. She turned and looked up at the rose bushes grown tall in her absence. A bird or animal must have caused the petals to fall in this long curve, she thought.

The trail led to her own fence, to a small bone with ants marching around it. Pink flesh hung off the marrow. Perhaps it was a hawk or one of the kites, or a ferret that had ruffled the bushes and set down there to eat. She turned around to the trail before her, long and gold, and was suddenly struck. *Oh no, no. Not now, not now.* The tears, the heaving chest, the throb in the heart. There was no reason rose-petals should have had this effect on her. There was nothing about roses that recalled him.

But she had just glimpsed him. In this lemon-coloured trail, laid, perhaps, to say good-morning, how are you today, I am free, I am happy, I am indeed *in the next room*. She took a deep breath, returned inside and walked resolutely towards the bedroom.

She entered quickly, looking over at the bed (he was not there, sleeping or reading). She saw head and leg indents, where, she remembered, he had gone for a nap before they had left the house all those months ago. She went to pull up the blind. As the light poured into the room, she caught a glint of light reflected off the golden Buddha on the dressing table. From the window she could see the side of the sanctuary, the Cooley hills, Ramsey's tall trees crowned with crows' nests, the rocky tufts of Ramsey's field. Sometimes from this window they had watched men with long guns roam in and out of that field looking for grouse or rabbits. And sometimes, during the day, young hawks and eaglets would be trained with string around bits of meat. The two fields looked so similar. An uneven gorse hedge with lots of gaps seemed to be the only divide between life in one, and death in the other. How they wished they could have erected warning signs for the animals that might wander in the wrong direction.

She turned to the Buddha, touched its golden head. He had never practiced. He claimed to have forgotten, too, the rules of his two birth religions (Catholicism and Islam) so, instead, followed a simple bespoke ceremony. He laid out rosary beads on a white linen cloth, placed a black and white photograph of his father (sitting on a prayer-mat in Cairo) against a miniature of the Little Child of Prague given to him by his mother, and lit candles. Certainly, he spoke to something or someone when he came in here and sat by the dressing table. She never thought to ask him what, or whom, exactly. She knew only that she would find him in deep commune with it, or them, and that he would cry with his eyes closed, rocking back and forth – then reach out and touch the statue or beads or photo as if reaching for a life raft.

Someone had been in. There were two thin drinking glasses filled with mayflowers on either side of the statue, and a tealight that had burned out. She touched the buds and put her fingers to her nose: a pineapple smell. Immediately, there they were, on cue, the burning tears. She blinked, forced them back. It must have been Mrs Ramsey. She had asked her to check the place, given her keys. Perhaps Mrs Ramsey had seen him sitting here through the window, and known completely what he was doing hunched over the statue, clutching at the beads and the photo of his father. It was the one part of their fight she had not shared; she did not know how to pray, nor what it was that one prayed to (the Humanist service had been her idea). Mrs Ramsey must know, or else she would not have left the flowers, now wilted, their heads almost bald. She collected them up, threw them in the bag she'd brought in with her, carried it into the hall.

She managed to fill three bags with out-of-date cosmetics, food products, wastepaper from the office, junk mail. She packed a crate with things she could recycle: newspapers, tins, bottles (a reminder of her heavy consumption of wine that winter). She would bring the bags and crate to the recycling centre in town. She lined up the green bags filled with pulses and rice and vitamin pills to give to her father. She was convinced now that she would put the house up for sale and return to London. It would be impossible to remain and carry on a life here. He was not here. He was not anywhere. Not in the bedroom sleeping or praying; not in the office drawing; not in the living-room staring out at the grouse and peacocks; not by the garage imagining the spa. He had vanished. Truly, he had passed away. Into that sweet-jar-shaped canister of ashes held in the office at the crematorium (waiting for her to make up her mind – to scatter or to keep). And she'd better stop this looking, this being-revealed-to business, because it was only a step away from stopping strangers on the street, to see if he had gone there, into the body of another man.

She picked up her handbag and rummaged inside for the keys to her car. She clutched at the cold bundle, placed them down on the long iroko shelf in the hallway (the brown-black colour of his Mediterranean eyes) and dropped the bag. She could not stop looking. If she had seen him in the rose-petals then he must be here. He would come to her. She needed a place to lie down. Her legs felt weak. Weightless and frail, she drifted from side to side along the hall, aimlessly brushing up against the walls, mindlessly touching the edges of paintings – the Patrick Caulfields, the Paolozzis. She knew where she would end up: in the pit of tears that would tear at her ribs and rip her throat. She opened the bedroom door, glided towards her side of the bed, slipped under the duvet and the folded-down throw, and turned to cradle the indents.

An hour must have passed this way. When she woke she recalled she had not seen his face (as in a dream), or had any memory of him, but had been overcome, bombarded with colours: blacks and blues, deep greens and golds. She'd been tossed from one shade to the next, had emitted fluctuating levels of cries, until, at rest, jaded and empty she landed on *yellow*, and here she breathed easy, stroking his pillow rhythmically, till her mind cleared, whereupon she fell into a deep sleep.

A voice came from outside, by the window. She was sure she could be seen curled up on the dishevelled, tear-soaked bed like a child. She went onto her knees and looked out. Mrs Ramsey had begun her retreat towards Cotter's Lane. She jumped up, ran out of the room and opened the front door.

'Mrs Ramsey, Clare, Clare – I'm in, it's me, I'm home.' Mrs Ramsey turned and walked towards her with her head bowed.

'I'm sorry love, I'm so sorry.' Mrs Ramsey reached out and hugged her, then rubbed her arms vigorously up and down, passing into her skin from hard warty hands, motherliness, and a heartfelt sympathy. Then, with tears in her eyes, she asked if there was anything she could do.

'No. Not for the moment.'

Mrs Ramsey said nothing when she told her Chalfont was to be sold, that she could no longer see herself living here now her husband was gone. Mrs Ramsey seemed to understand.

'Thank you for the mayflowers.'

'Oh, that was your father. Saw him pick them along the Lane. He's awfully put out. He wanted to go over, but the journey would have been too much for him, you know that.'

She closed the door. She looked in the hall mirror, at her face, lined and black-streaked, at the slate-coloured weariness around her eyes. Fixing her fuzzy hair, she remembered she had not pulled down the blinds. Inside the bedroom she straightened the duvet, folded down the throw, removed the damp pillow. She would place it on her bed in the house tonight; it still had his smell, clean and powdery, of the woods after a night's rain, and there were a few grey hairs still clinging. She pulled down the blind and closed the door, brought the pillow to the pile of things in the hall ready to be loaded into the Jeep. She went into the office, pulled down the blinds, brushed her hand along the row of tall, dusty books on modern architecture as she exited, and closed the door.

She stared out at the sanctuary; it rustled in parts and she thought she saw the hare, but couldn't make it out amongst the rocks and deadwood. She had become out of step with the movements of the place. Once, they were attuned to the darting of a grouse here, a rabbit there. The animals were so quick, so adept at camouflaging themselves (except for the flagrant prowling of the ferret who would steal in without caring who or what observed him), that only a kind of hawk-eyed seeing could follow their progress through all that scrub. After months of such looking even the nightlit grass had become penetrable.

She knew if she stared long enough the green undulating veil would lift, and she would see that wild world once more. Maybe tomorrow. Tomorrow she would come back to this house whose name he had not wanted to change, sit in this room with a cup of tea, and look out at the fields. Or, if not tomorrow then the next day, whenever she was ready to look steadily into things, for she was not able to do so now. She thought of her father, and wondered what he'd like to eat for lunch. There would be things to do for him; she would need to go to the shops. Today, if he let her, she would treat him to a meal in a restaurant in town. The day was fine. It would be really lovely, she thought, to walk.

Clare Counting

STEVE DEARDEN

She swims sixty lengths a day or thereabouts. Thereabouts because however Clare counts, she becomes unsure whether she is on length thirteen or eleven or maybe fifteen, or if on an even length – fourteen, sixteen or twelve.

When she started swimming again Clare tried bending back a finger for each length, but rolled like a stroke victim so counted every two lengths rather than one, then tried imagining beads on an abacus, but she always lost count around twelve, again round twenty-six, the mid thirties, early forties. So some days she may well swim six or eight extra lengths, or two or four less than she set out to, though this is unlikely as she is anxious not to cheat herself.

Clare tries a new technique, darkening the grout under a new tile with water every other length. She swims a slick cap and goggled crawl, but is sick of being mown through in the fast lanes by men who don't look up.

If anyone were to ask her what was the most important thing in her life, Clare would say this swim every weekday at 6am then laugh – of course Eric her partner and their daughter Lia were more important – but having forced their move from the hills to live scrunched up on top of each other in the middle of the city, she knew she would break apart without a daily thrash of water and counting.

So, the end of their first week in the new apartment, Clare sat Eric down at their tiny glass table set into the wall of the galley kitchen and said, 'I will go mad unless I swim.' He surprised her, agreeing to get Lia up, ready and to nursery in the mornings, saying 'Fine, no problem, we don't want you going mad on us,' and did the thing he does when something seems obvious to him and he wants to move on, twisting round his wrist with forefinger and thumb as if tightening a seal.

*

Two months into their new life, learning how to live in a city for the first time, Eric still feels as if he is on holiday. Just before the move he completed a contract big enough for him to spend six months looking for work he wants rather than has to do. So he pushes Lia to her nursery in the basement of a converted chapel, buys a paper. The boyish blond barista with a pierced cheek and tattoos has his black coffee poured before he reaches her station, hovers her plastic pincers between the plain croissant and the iced swirl, knowing he has begun to worry about his weight.

From his table in the window Eric still gets a buzz looking up at their apartment, like a green glass cube accidentally left on top of an eight storey Victorian conversion. Their space is big floor to ceiling but small in square footage, just three rooms, in two of which – Lia's and the bathroom – he is conscious of his elbows, the other a great open space: living area, kitchen, the mezzanine Eric and Clare sleep on, cubby holes for wardrobes. All their clutter from the cottage is in charity shops or stored in containers stacked in a mid Pennine mill. Eric feels sleek despite his waistline, feels focused even though he has no idea what exactly he is going to do next.

Every morning since the move Eric has delayed going back to the dry putty and new wood smells, back to his desk tucked under the stairs. Today, as usual, he grazes among the shops, finds a postcard of their block in the nineteenth century and, seduced by wide greens and blues, buys a book of photographs looking down on the world. After wandering into a boutique to check out their marble floor, he follows a couple into a jewellers next door where he remembers Clare needs a watch. The display cabinets contain only fronds of blue and scarlet dried grass, artificial birds of paradise perched on dead branches. When a girl in a dark trouser suit asks what he is interested in, he realizes this is not a jeweller for browsing, but one where they bring out trays from the back of the shop and all the sales people have clear plastic earpieces.

Eric wants to damage things, be rude. He leaves and makes for home gently humiliated, overwhelmed with love for Lia. On Saturday, the day Lia is two, Eric will be forty-four. The mathematical symmetry seems a good omen, he feels less good thinking the day she is eighteen he will be sixty.

Wired on caffeine he stands in the thin rain trying to get his keycard to swipe. He presses through the buzzers until he finds a neighbour home to let him in, takes the stairs rather than the lift, resents how they always fool him – the times he is tired there is suddenly one more flight to their door, but when he dashes up, Eric arrives at their apartment a flight early, still full of running.

★

Clare specialises in professional malpractice, defending lawyers against lawyers. She knows she shouldn't talk work with Eric because he is twisting at his wrists, he has played with Lia, put her to bed, there are a couple of beer cans and foil takeaway cartons on his desk and, trying to shut her up so he can watch the ten o'clock news, he says, 'Just tell them you don't like her approach. Better now than when it goes belly up.'

'Don't always tell me what to do.'

'Then don't ask me.'

'I wasn't asking, I just want you to go "there there".'

'There there.'

'You don't mean that.' She nips the end off her cigarette, runs the stub under the tap, bins it. 'I thought we had noodles.'

'There. *There!* Right in front of you.'

'Ha ha.' Clare disagrees with the strategy that Sue, her boss, is taking. She knows, but decides not to share with Eric, that she is keeping quiet because Sue is the only other woman lawyer in the firm.

He comes and perches on a stool at the glass table. 'You're keeping schtum because she's the only other woman.'

'Don't talk shit.'

Clare pushes his shoulder so she can open the fridge for ready made black bean sauce. 'Sue's admitting too much.'

'There there.'

'She's too anxious to compromise.'

'There there.'

'Fuck off. Right this is nearly ready.'

Clare lights another cigarette, ducks under the hob's hood and waits for Eric to say, *You smoke too much, I can't understand why you have to smoke right before eating, you ruin your taste.*

Tonight he says, 'I picked up this leaflet, I thought at the weekend we could go across, take the train.'

She says, 'Lovely.' Though she would rather bounce around the apartment all weekend, catching up with herself. 'Lovely. Do they have dolphins? Don't look at me like that, honestly – it'll be lovely.'

'You look good, is it the swimming or the fags?'

Clare puts her hand on her stomach almost as flat as it once was. She feels heavy and for a moment she has to turn away so Eric can't see her face.

After she has eaten they watch the news from the top again, then make love on the sofa. Maybe because they lack a wall to define the bedroom, their lovemaking has spilled into the lounge, even the tiny kitchen and, unlike in the old house, they make love before what Eric calls her 'rigmarole'.

She watches *Sex and the City* until she hears him dragging breath round his tongue up on the mezzanine, has a cigarette under the cooker hood, goes into the bathroom to start her rigmarole and thinks about what she would do if she was leading on the case, what to get Lia and Eric for their birthday, what to get Lia to give to her father, 'hears' Eric saying *No wonder you sleep so badly, you have such a rigmarole of creams and potions and staring in the mirror that you wake yourself up.* Clare pushes the balls of her hands into her forehead until she is able to leave the bathroom, turn down the lights. In the green glass glow of the city she walks lengths of the apartment, does her facial exercises, irons the crumpled skirt and a new shirt for the morning, packs her swimming bag, has another cigarette and looks at the case papers, pacing the space, glad of the dark sky and that they are higher than the buildings around them. Lights another cigarette but almost immediately douses it under the tap.

Lia's tiny room hasn't a window, which worries Clare. Eric has talked about painting a faux view, maybe he will now he has less work on. She kisses her fingers and lays them on Lia's forehead thinking how Eric doesn't tell Lia things, just asks her too many questions, *What's that? Do you want this or that? What colour's this? How many are there? Is this a fish or a lion?* With her he is all answers no questions and when she says, *You are so sure of everything,* he replies, *I only say what I think. I might be wrong. You might be right.* He is always so certain. *Certainly. But I may be wrong.* Until now Clare has never been sure whether Eric was wrong in his conviction that they should not have another child. Now she is certain.

She goes into the bathroom rubs moisturiser into her face, pulling her skin back from her cheek bones, chin. One of the things she has never told Eric is that she has been in this building before. She must have been eight or nine when her father, a buyer for a textile firm, brought her onto one of the floors below, rows of women at machines, dust hanging in the noise. Lying beside Eric the nights she can't sleep, the buzz of the air conditioner is thousands of shirts being cut and sewn, and the women's lips silently shouting across their machines to each other.

★

Eric drops Lia at nursery, gives the caffeine a miss, buys a paper and a lottery ticket for the Saturday draw. Friends give him flak for supporting the 'poor tax' but, like increasing numbers of them, much of his income comes from projects paid for by the Lottery. If he wins he will build his own house half way up the hill outside their old village. Eric tucks the ticket under his desk lamp base with all the unchecked others, resists opening his email and begins to feed last month's expenditure into his cash flow. His mobile rings softly from between the cushions on the sofa.

'Now then Eric, it's Alan Bourne, I want to pick your brain.'

Eric pictures long podgy red fingers, Bourne's sandy hair, their one previous contact three years back, a quick drink at a trade fair when Bourne had been an agent for one of the big firms and Eric one of only three or four consultants sourcing his range of tiles and marble. Nowadays hardly a month goes by without someone *just giving him a ring* to say they're making the jump, going freelance themselves. Then the *just picking your brain* calls start.

'I want something that reflects but isn't reflective, is resistant but the environment I've got is fairly benign, maybe Telic but I don't want that metal effect, I want something glasslike but not glass, Sistra or that kind of inter-layered stuff, you know what I mean?'

Eric pokes his toe under the sofa and drags out Clare's bra, holds the phone down by his waist. Since moving here he always seems to be fucking Clare in her work clothes. At first he put this down to the way spaces spill into each other in the apartment, but there is also a new sharp edge in Clare that he feels her rubbing against him, maybe something left from the rows about having another child, or this new environment among stores and offices that are empty at night.

He hears a small, distant voice, 'Eric? Eric? Eric mate?'

Eric hasn't found a way of charging for his brain being picked, or claiming against tax for what falls somewhere between favours owed, being an industry player, conversations maybe leading to work, and off-pissing. He wants to say, *Do you read the trade journals? The internet? Everybody's talking about exactly what you want.* He saw the invitation to tender for the job Bourne is doing, the money was shit and they got it.

'Look, email me, I'm with my daughter just now, I'll get back to you.'

And immediately a text message. From Jean, the motherly P.A. to his old Chief Exec. *Ring me pls asap.*

He jabs, scrolls, jabs, prepares to turn her down, explain how working for John McClaren again would be a backwards step, 'Jean, it's Eric.'

'Bad news I'm afraid, but I am sure you would want to know, the night before last, John died.'

'Jean I'm...' Eric searches for a word, he is not surprised, not shocked, people die, and sometimes he knows them.

'They were eating at that Italian they go to, with Sheila and the kids, he went to the loo and didn't come back, Sheila asked one of the waiters and they found him. I don't know more, there's an inquest on Monday. Oh Eric, be careful, he can only have been a little older than you.'

'Younger actually.'

'All those poor children, they were celebrating the twins' birthday. What a way. I'll do an email when I know about the funeral. I expect I'll see you there then.'

Eric thinks, *No you won't.* The idea of standing around

being complimentary about McClaren invades the balance and stretch he has found since the move to the city and the promise he made to himself to only do things for the right reasons. He picks up Clare's bra and goes up on to the mezzanine, takes picture books and toys from their bed through into Lia's room. Clare is right, the tall, narrow box needs something to give Lia's eyes length. Eric imagines a frame on the wall, how if he punched through there would be a roof-scape of skylights, lift plant, air conditioning units, and beyond them the hills, sheep, stone walls, trees, flowers, cliffs, beaches, gulls, fish, liners, Denmark, Sweden, Latvia, Russia.

★

Clare's team and the client hang around in the smoky court canteen waiting for the case to be called. Their brittle grey-skinned clerk keeps coming back to croak messages, *He's in chambers, something urgent.* Mid morning it's, *He's doing sentencing left over from last week.* At lunch time, *He's got a stomach bug, put us off 'til Monday.*

David, the barrister, picks at the crease in his wool trousers and says, 'Meaning golf weekend.'

In the taxi back to the office, Clare wonders how Sue's skin breathes through her shiny lacquer make-up, how if not for Botox she'd have thin lips that would slice whatever she said. Clare has not fathomed her new boss yet – sometimes she will be laddish and jokey, open a bottle of wine to close meetings that have gone well, rib the married men that they will never make it because they want to go home and the single guys that they need homes and women to go to. Other times she will shut them all out so they have to play games to suss how she feels about lines, positions, strategies they propose, remaining aloof and brooding – what Clare suspects Sue thinks is enigmatic, but comes across as petulant. No one in the office can or will tell Clare anything about Sue's private life.

Back at her desk, Clare taps her finger along the labels on the shelf's worth of box files for a case pending and blocks out Eric's *Start as you mean to go on, draw the lines or they'll walk all over you.* She pulls down a file, begins to sift and weigh. At four-thirty, reckoning she has worked enough to spike Eric's advice and satisfy her conscience, she goes looking for birthday presents. She is incisive, within fifteen minutes Eric will get a shirt and a book of pictures looking down on the world, Lia a doll, a doctor's set in a plastic briefcase, a set of Nemo characters, she also buys wrapping paper and labels, then goes looking for something Lia can give Eric. She walks past a bar called Blue and sees him sitting at a table with a bottle of Budweiser and a pile of magazines. Rings him,

'Hi it's me.'

'Hi, how are you?'

'You working?'

'Yes, catching up on trade journals.'

'There's a number on the pad on your desk, I wonder if you could get it for me.'

'Um.' She hears his cogs whirring, 'No I'm in a bar actually.'

'In a bar. OK.'

There must be something in her voice that makes him look up, seeing her he grins, his head dips on his shoulders shy and caught out, she sees how he hasn't always been a big man.

'Come and join me.'

She has a coffee, blows out her first long drag of smoke in a tight whistling sigh.

'What do you want from Lia?'

'My God, I don't know, just to be ha-'

'I mean for your birthday.'

'One of those small Bentleys.'

Clare shows Eric the presents she bought for Lia. The racks of blue bottles behind the bar remind them of Greece, the sea, Clare holds the big stone of her ring up to the light, the exact colour. Slowly they become delighted by the surprise of each other's week day company and touch finger-end to finger-end, the inside of each other's forearms, lean in shoulders, foreheads.

Eric says, 'I was looking at my figures today, thinking maybe I could go away with Lia for a week, Lerici maybe, there's a couple of work things, but most of the time we could just go to the beach, and you come out for a long weekend. What do you think? Maybe the end of next month.'

Clare takes her hands back, 'OK.'

'You mind?'

'Of course not, good idea.'

Eric often argued how the freedom to take off on such trips would be exactly what they would lose with a second child. Clare finds this almost unbearably selfish.

'You sure you don't mind?'

'Of course I mind, I want to come but I can't take a holiday this soon in the job.' For Clare there is the deeper shadow of how, when Eric had taken Lia to Holland with his parents, a child had come, just not the right child.

He thumbs the torn strips of Budweiser foil into rumples on the wet bottle, 'McClaren died yesterday, at Gino's. He went to pee and didn't come back. What do you think that is like? Dying alone in a toilet knowing your kids are in the next room?'

Clare looks at her wrist, 'Shit. What's the time?'

'Stay here for a while, read your magazine, you relax, I'll collect her, we could –'

'Let's both go.'

'Clare, I wish we had had Lia earlier in our lives.'

'We didn't know each other earlier in our lives, and in any case –'

'..she wouldn't be Lia –'

'..if she was born earlier. No.'

★

Trying to chop carrots quietly, Eric can hear Clare on their mezzanine bed lowering and lengthening her story-reading voice to draw Lia into drowsiness. Lia is talking to the stuffed cat they have been trying to get her to name.

'Cat, cat, catty cat, cat Mummy, cat, catty cat.'

'You can't call a cat cat.'

'Catty cat.'

'Lia, are you listening to this story or not?'

On silent mode, Eric's mobile buzzes across and nearly off their glass table.

'Eric, it's Sheila, Sheila McClaren.'

'Jean rang me. I'm...' Eric still hasn't located a word.

'There was no sign Eric, he just got up from the table and went, he looked very peaceful, not like he had been in pain or anything, the restaurant people were very good, they had a first responder, tried to revive him, but.'

Eric realises he is whispering. 'If there's anything I can do.'

Sheila mirrors him, quiet and husky, 'Well there is actually, which is why I am ringing, I've been discussing this with his family, we want someone who knew John well through work to speak at the funeral.'

'When is it?'

'Well the inquest's on Monday but the doctor seems pretty sure it was an aneurism, if the inquest goes according to... if the doctor's right, then we have pencilled in Thursday. Rawdon.'

'I'm sorry Sheila.' As he lies to her, Eric regrets treating Sheila McClaren as he did Alan Bourne and his reflective but non reflective metallic glass. 'I have this trip planned. Italy. With my daughter.'

'That's a shame.'

'I'm sorry. We've had it booked some time now, she's... you know.'

'She's too young to be disappointed.'

'Yes. And there's business stuff fixed too.'

'We have people from the Sailing Club, Scouts, Rotary speaking, everyone I have spoken to says you are the man to do it.'

'I'm sorry.' Eric feels he would like to give more to Sheila McClaren. The few times he had met her at work parties, he had admired and been turned on by her straightforward way of talking to people she met rarely or for the first time. He imagines she will marry again soon, at her own pace and successfully.

'No, Eric, you take... sorry I have forgotten her name.'

'Lia.'

'Take Lia, whereabouts in Italy?'

'Lerici.'

'Vespas and beach umbrellas, you expect Claudia Cardinale to come round the corner in a convertible, watch out there's something very unpleasant happens mid-morning on the centre of the free beach there, very brown, I'd pay if I were you. It will be lovely this time of year.'

'Thank you Sheila.'

'I'm sure you will be thinking of us, on the day.'

Clare creeps from the mezzanine, Lia sleeping in her arms, mouths 'Liar.'

Eric mouths 'Lawyer' back at her, switches off his phone, unplugs the kettle and plugs in the charger. He watches the battery icon fill up and empty, fill up and empty. The vegetables are chopped, a yellow sodium haze comes up from the streetlamps below, he crushes a garlic clove knowing the heavy Wüsthof knife will outlast him, as will his wedding ring, his chromatic sheets and piles of sample tiles, stones, marbles – things Lia will have to decide whether to keep or throw out. Switching on the hood fan he knows the apartment will fill with cooking anyway. When Clare comes from Lia he pours her wine and she teases him for lying.

'They asked me to speak at the funeral. What am I supposed to say, sorry, actually Sheila I couldn't stand John?'

'He seemed a lovely man.'

'McClaren! No, he was a bully, he couldn't give a fuck, it was all cost, margin, screw the other guy, you know this, you must have known.'

'You never showed it.'

'Whether I liked him or not is irrelevant. A couple of months ago I would have gone, put the suit on, worked the audience... audience? Congregation? Mourners?... dragged tears from them, wouldn't matter if it was true or not. But not now, I'm not being dragged into things I don't want now, I'm trying to hold on to something here.'

Clare is poised, her glass to but not touching her lips, waiting for him to say more, to describe what that something might be. There is no more, that's it. He expects her to say, *Me too* and talk about another child for Lia, he expects her to use phrases like *a proper family*. Eric gets up and switches the hob fan off, opens the oven and buries the possibility of a conversation in assembling their meal.

★

Clare knows she has not slept since they went to bed. If she were to nudge Eric from the rasp of his snoring, he would tell her that she had not been awake as long as she thought and that she has drifted in and out of sleep. Clare is certain. She has been thinking about Lia and her room, about the impossibly enormous quote for curtains or blinds on the big green windows, just how misguided Botox Sue's case strategy is, which clothes she will need to pack for the House of Lords hearing next week, how to stop Eric's snoring, thinking about her age and another child and whether the gritty feeling in her womb is real. Balling up each of her thoughts she distributes them around her body, in her ankles, neck, shoulders, stomach. She has tried all her usual tricks – yoga, valerian tea, meditation, counting lengths, vodka, but in the ambient city light she can clearly make out Eric's watch the other side of the bed – three forty-five.

She tosses and turns heavily, deliberately. Slams her shoulder and head into the mattress, then the ball in her neck bursts – Clare elbows Eric in the back.

'I can't sleep.'

'Mm?'

'I can't sleep, why won't Lia go down in her room?'

'Oh – what?'

'Why won't Lia go down in her room?'

'Give her time.'

'You were going to paint that view.'

'I will, I will.'

Clare sits up, throws off the duvet, 'Then it's no good trolling about in bars and coffee shops, you could have done it by now.'

'OK.'

'She hates that room.'

'She wants stories here because you make such a thing about her having them in there –'

'She'll hate this whole flat if you don't paint her a view soon.'

'OK – what shall I paint – office blocks, a shopping centre?'

'See, moving here was a mistake, you hate it too.'

'I don't.'

'Why say that if you don't?'

'A joke, for fuck's sake.' Eric gives in and sits up, heaving the duvet back over his legs, 'I'll paint her sheep, ducks, sailing boats, fish, don't worry. Clare, I love it here, I'm glad we've done it –'

'But?'

'No buts, no buts.'

'If we had another –'

'We're not going to have another.'

'Says who?'

'Oh so this is what… why bring it all… I thought we'd agreed.'

'You thought we agreed Eric.'

'We discussed it.'

'We haven't finished discussing it.'

For a few seconds they sit staring at their reflections in opposite windows.

Clare gets out of bed, 'It's no good, I'm getting up to work for a while.'

'So that's... you're thinking about bloody Sue again.'

'No. I wasn't.'

'Just tell her the bloody truth.'

'Like you telling Sheila McClaren the bloody truth.'

All the balls of thought churn Clare's stomach. As she closes the bathroom door she hears Eric say 'I'm confused' meaning *I am tired, I'm going to sleep. Let's leave it 'til morning,* meaning *never.* As she is being sick Clare knows that he won't want to talk in the morning, and that she will be racing thoughts all night. She spits, cleans her teeth, uses Lia's wipes round her lips and nose, smell masking smell and the taste of vomit, chlorine in the pit of her throat. Feeling queasy again she kneels over the toilet, waiting for the nausea to pass, the bathroom fan to slow down, the rattle and thrum of thousands of sewing machines to cease.

★

Five a.m. on the birthday Saturday Clare has thought her way into believing her case strategy is the only one that will work. She slips out of bed, clears last night's plate and glasses from the floor around the sofa and while waiting for her laptop to boot, checks Lia, makes espresso. Clare writes an email to Sue, then goes back cutting out where she has over-reached, erasing her angry snipes, her flippant passion, crafts a package of sense, reason, lucidity, precedent. She hits *Send* and sits back wanting to settle in this capsule of knowing she is good, needful of nothing.

Lia comes running in, 'Mummy, mummy, mummy.'

Stuffing Tigger into Clare's lap, 'Boing. Boing. Boing.'

'Happy Birthday.'

Lia sings nearer to a tune than she has ever been, 'Happy Birthday to you, Happy Birthday to you, Happy Birthday to..'

'Lia and Daddy.'

'To Lia and Daddy and Mummy and Tigger and Lia and Grandpa and Mouse and Lia and –'

'Happy.'

'Birthday to you.'

They wake Eric, tear wrapping paper, Eric puts on his shirt, Lia listens to their hearts through her stethoscope, takes her new doll's temperature, then gives them all injections. They agree to give one of the books of photos looking down on the world to Clare's sister. Luckily Eric is delighted that his present from Lia is a set of Nemo characters and is happy to share them. Lia takes Nemo and Dory downstairs to watch their video. While Lia explains to the fish what will happen to them next, Clare rolls on her side, ready for sleep now, balanced in the excellence of her email to Sue. Eric spoons in behind her.

'You want a reward just for being forty-four?'

'Mmm.'

She touches him idly like trailing her fingers in slow water, their night-time row is still too full in her chest. 'I'm sorry. No.' She can feel him holding tense, wondering whether to push things, then he gives in though lies still spooned in her back hoping she might change her mind.

They have breakfast at the station and cross the hills to the coast. As soon as they get off the train, Lia wants to get back on again. Clare and Eric try and convince her.

'But we are going to see the fish.'

'An aquarium, big tanks of fish.'

'Sharks and whales.'

'Whales!'

'I don't think they have whales, maybe little ones, Belugas maybe.'

'Luga whales.'

'Yes Belugas.'

'See lugas.'

'And rays, big flat fish.'

'Fat fish?'

'Flat fish.'

'Fat Lugas.'

They are all laughing now.

'Where's that shuttle bus?'

'Cuttle fish.'

'Where did she get cuttle fish from?'

'God knows.'

'Parrots maybe.'

'Parrots there!'

Eric and Clare together, 'No!'

The aquarium lifts are out of order, so there are extra attendants on hand to guide people up and down the walkways. They make a great fuss helping them angle Lia's three-wheeled buggie into the flow of people coming up from the big tank, asking Lia if it was her first time here, telling her how much she will enjoy herself.

Lia shows them her own fish, chanting 'Nemo and Dory, Nemo and Dory, Nemo and Dory. Birthday fish.'

'Oh lovely, how old?'

'Forty-four.'

'It's his birthday too.'

'Both today! How wonderful, and how old are you little one, mm?'

'Two.'

'Amazing!'

'Nemo and Dory, Nemo and Dory.'

In the dark round the huge central aquarium, Lia loses her chatter, transfixed by the slow silent spin of fish, the sharks with their long thin lieutenants sucked onto their backs, bellies, shoals of silver oval tiles swimming one way then tilting *en masse* the other, rays criss-crossing the bottom in swoops. Eric stands back with his camera, trying to capture Clare and Lia, heads leaning close into each other and the tank life spread behind them. He gets nothing but silhouettes and luminous green.

A dive of bubbles draws light down from the tank surface, long blonde hair streaming from a mask and flipper kick. The girl swims round behind and slightly under the sharks, then rolls herself over inspecting the stub of a tail, selects her next fish, kicks round, behind, under, over the wake, her task different from anything Eric knows about, wild and beautiful. He moves close to the glass, takes a photograph. Looking at the real girl circling in the huge volume of water, then in the small tank on his camera screen he feels sticky hot and claustrophobic.

They move on, the girl swims beside him, she is a miniature diver in the tanks of tropicals, she lolls on the surface of the lagoon area, her wet breath buzzes his ear as he tries to take in the wall texts, the videos of ice shattering, whales surfacing and rolling back under, she sits dripping beside them while they eat their non-fishy lunch, when Eric goes over to look through the café's high prow window she waves from far out in the muddy estuary.

*

Clare is too tired to stop Lia pouring juice from her carton onto the sauce smeared plates, into the empty sandwich packets and yogurt pots. On the other side of the restaurant three couples and their children are making the kind of noise reserved for amazing magic tricks or feats of startling bravery. A man with thick black hair and a pink boyish face that makes him look thirty not fifty is holding court, making up a story with two plastic fish. Clare is not sure how he does it, but Jeremy is sitting beside her almost immediately while back at his table they do not seem to have noticed him leaving.

'Clare.'

'Hello.'

He looks at her as if he has asked a question she has to answer, Clare lifts Lia onto her knee, jolting Jeremy into commonplace, 'Hello little one. So how's the new job then?'

'Fine.'

'Sue Jenck not driving you mad?'

'Not yet, we'll see.'

'And you, how are you?'

Eric comes back from the window and takes the wriggling Lia off Clare's knee, holds her a little too tight.

'Eric, this is Jeremy Hobbs, was at Crawford Milner Roe with me, Jeremy, my husband.'

The men shake hands like they would each gladly drown the other in a sack. Clare wishes Jeremy would go. He is part of her story Eric knows nothing of. She sees it as cold information, a slow evolutionary diagram unfolding on one of the aquarium video screens. How, with Eric and Lia in Holland, she had found in Jeremy the sheer relief of spending time with a man who did not project certainty like Eric, and understood that equivocation was erotic, temporary dishonesty one of love's techniques.

While the men struggle to make conversation Clare looks at the plastic cutlery, the mess of orange, yoghurt and tissues on the tray, mud out in the estuary. She has no evidence, other than this feeling of grit in her womb, that the abortion removed more than the foetus. But of the fact that she is no longer able to conceive, she is now certain. She takes Eric gently by his upper arm.

'Come on, we must be on our way.'

★

Sitting on the train home, tired and gazing along the great suspension bridge disappearing into the estuary fog, Eric is confusing the girl with Lia, a fish, his sperm, the light swimming away from him. He is wishing he could accelerate

Lia's life, grieving for all the things she will do that he will miss. The thought of dying like McClaren, of leaving Lia is almost unbearable. He wants to tell Clare he knows this is absurd, he wants to ask her how can you be lonely when you are dead and slowly moves his thumb and forefinger tips from side to side on the table between himself and Lia stretched asleep across two seats.

Eric and Clare each wait for the other to speak.

Clare can feel Eric's shoulder on hers, she is not leaning on him, but she does not want to break the contact either. She watches the estuary curve away from them, land filling the inbetween, they become surrounded by fields and, in the distance, hills. She is not prepared to think about the past and cannot bear to imagine the future, when she gets home she will have to work late preparing for the Lords hearing but suppresses all detail now. She knows she will one day apologise to Lia, even if she is not quite sure now exactly what she will be apologising for, and for whom, her? Eric? They sidle through a city, then through more hills, a couple of valleys north lies the fold in which their old village, their old life is tucked.

Lia shifts in her sleep and turns away from them and the soft beluga whale toy on the table Clare buries her hand in and kneads. Closing her eyes she imagines herself reaching for the pool edge, turning, kicking away off the tiles, counting.

Eric starts, 'Sorry?'

'Nothing.'

They are both trying not to think about what happened leaving the aquarium. The girl on the shop till had helped them down the ramps when they arrived. 'Big one forty-six, little one two, see I remember, did you have a good time?'

Eric paid for the soft beluga, 'Forty-four actually.'

'And how did the other little one do?'

Eric struggled to find the right coins, 'What?'

'Sweet little thing, gorgeous.'

'You're mixing us up with someone else.'

'No, I'm sure you had.' The girl had a lovely, open face. She looked to Clare, 'The baby, you had the little boy with you.'

'No,' said Clare, 'There was no baby.'

Lector

DAVID ROSE

A goat coughed on the path above the roof, but he read on unwavering, his tone undiminished, the old man beating time with his slippered foot.

In fact he was not so much reading as reciting, having read this memoir now countless times. It was, besides, a vanity reading – the memoir having been ghostwritten for the old man years before – and in his professional pride he rather despised the task. But it had to be done and, since the old man was an insomniac and the reading early, he could treat it as a warm-up for his larynx before the real workday began. So he could stretch his vocal cords, burnish his tone, practice his pitch and pace and emphatic stress while his auditor, eyes closed, recited along with him under his breath, alert only to deviances from text, all lectoral subtleties lost.

They had now reached the *hot gates* and *blood-drenched reeds*; he was on the home straight, having to restrain the imperceptible acceleration.

At last they reached *safe harbour* on a diminuendo even he was pleased with, and he put down the redundant script.

Refusing as usual the salted porridge and coffee, he got through the adieus and pulled on his gloves. He wheeled his moped to the road, yanked on the starting string and mounted.

The bungs behind the gravel pits were greening, the birds return-ing, the sun shining on the gravel mounds: spring barging in.

He ventured his nose above the windshield to fill his lungs, flex his diaphragm, gargle with the spring air.

There were two hours before his first official reading at the Community Centre. He decided to treat himself to breakfast. He turned off the engine, coasted into the car park of the café, padlocked his moped to a tree.

Reluctantly he decided against the black pudding – he couldn't risk heartburn on lectoral duty – chose an egg on toast and coffee with free refills, of which he availed himself twice. This gave him the chance to prepare.

He took his file from his pouch, spreading the contents on the table. It was the usual parish business; minutes and decisions from the last council meeting, local league football results, notice of impending drain clearances. But nothing was beneath contempt; the humblest handbill deserved coherence, clarity and accurate emphasis. This had been instilled into them on the training programme under the Work-For-Poets Initiative, but accorded in any case with his personal sense of professionalism.

He quickly scanned them – a silent reconnoitre – then went back and rehearsed in an unvoiced reading, marking the stresses in pencil, practising the pronunciations (many of the council officials were unusually named). Satisfied, he leaned back and enjoyed a fourth coffee.

The hall was filling up as he arrived, most of the village attending for the free refreshments the Government had provided, and by the time he had padlocked his moped, removed his goggles and gloves and combed his hair, the audience was full strength.

He began reading at once.

He read the minutes of the last council meeting while the audience settled, finishing their tea, finding their glasses, moved onto the football scores to stir them to attention, then

on to the informative notices – the drain clearance programme, heard in sceptical silence, then on to the monthly
refusal of the requested bus shelter, again routine. He hadn't
even needed to rehearse it, being identically worded to last
month's refusal. But protocol dictated it be read. It provoked
a rash of outrage.

But his reading had been fluid, emphases and inflections
correct, unexaggerated, a text-book performance.

Still the indignation seethed. First one, then others
demanded he read it again.

He read slowly, resonantly, as neutrally as he could. It
provoked them even more. Who did the council think they
were talking to, children? Not content with seeing old people
soaked to the skin, they added sarcasm to their disregard.
They had previously been apologetic at least, now they were
blatant, adamant in their anti-populism. Protest was needed,
direct action proposed: golf umbrellas to be purchased, the
bill sent to the council; the bus to be blockaded, the driver
held in the hall... He was instructed to convey their
indignation to the committee involved. In vain, his
explanation that the texts were delivered to the Library, from
which he collected them the evening before.

He packed his pouch, gathered his things. A matronly
woman – the Matron of the adjacent Home – insisted on him
having another drink, to prepare him for the journey.

On his ride back to town he began to have his doubts about
what he had regarded as a sinecure.

He arrived at the factory in good time despite his musings. He
washed his face, adjusted the lectern and drew a cup of
filtered water as the workers filed in, chose their lunch.

This was a project he enjoyed, a full-blooded reading of
a proper book, part of the Urban Outreach Initiative – a
nostalgic return to live, human entertainment, a one-man
version of Workers' Playtime.

It was still in its early phase, but he had seen the book list for the first six months: Henry Green's *Living*, Sillitoe's *Saturday Night and Sunday Morning*, Mrs Gaskell's *North and South*. The strategy, so he guessed, was to subtly remind the workers of the bad old days, impress upon them the progress made in even non-I.T. industries.

They had therefore kicked off with a safe classic – Dickens' *Hard Times*. Something he could get his teeth into.

The clatter of cutlery trailed off as he coughed, opened the book, then his mouth.

Eschewing any pseudo-professional histrionics, he nonetheless warmed to the text, getting into the characters, distinguishing them rather by inflection and pitch than funny voices, employing a bass monotone for the background description, baritone for the homilies.

He had reached one of the relevant passages, describing the insanely nodding elephants of non-stop machinery, playing down its salience with skilful de-emphasis.

It was, despite that, and as hoped for, picked up on.

– We could do with a few bloody elephants in this place. Better than the crap we've got now. Forever bloody breaking down. Stop-go, stop-go. Fucking frustrating.

– Say what you like about the Victorians, they were damned good engineers. Their machinery's still in working order now.

– See that documentary last night about Kingdom Brunel?

– You mean the Kingdom of Brunei?

– I mean Brunel. Brunei's in South East Asia.

– My paper said Brunei.

– That's another skill that's gone to the dogs – proofreading. All bloody computers now with South Korean spellchecks. Probably made in Brunei.

He had, the while, been reading over this, lowering the

volume as instructed, to allow for the feedback. But there was no more comment, and he lifted the volume, concentrating on the accent of Stephen Blackpool.

When he got home his girlfriend was still there. She hadn't gone in to work. He detected some crestfall in her demeanour, asked, Aren't you well?

He made her some tea, offered to read to her in bed.

He peeked at the calendar as he poured the tea. There was no asterisk.

He carried the tea in, undressed, got in beside her, hoping if she were ill it wasn't infectious.

As if reading his thoughts, or at least his posture, she said It's alright, I'm not *ill* ill.

– Then what?

– It's neglect. I'm suffering from neglect.

When he awoke she was breathing slowly, probably asleep. He turned, his back to hers. With her warmth against him he was gently swelling. He drifted into fantasy, glad now to be the author of his own dreams. But as he gripped himself she stirred, turned.

– Kiss me then.

He was not on duty again until evening. The afternoon was his own. He decided to go to the park, freelance for a while.

He found a suitable tree with a bench nearby, hung his placard on the tree. Being sunny, there were plenty of people about. Many carried books.

A few drifted over, read the sign. It would take only one request to set off the others, overcome their embarrassment.

At last someone came up, handed him their book.

– How many pages do I get for a fiver?

He looked at it. Faulkner.

– Ten.

– That all? Bloke here last week did me twenty-five.

– Same book?

– No. A thriller. I'm eclectic.

– For a thriller I'd do you thirty. This is different. Longer sentences. Convoluted syntax. Ten's my standard. Eight for Henry James, five for Joyce. Alright, I'll do you twelve. My final offer.

– Done. Take a cheque?

– Where from?

– From the top.

He turned to the opening page, cleared his throat.

As he expected, this led to other requests. He spent the next hour and a half on a succession of books – fifty pages of Michel Faber, fifteen pages on John Grisham ('Only fifteen?' 'Tortuous prose.'), a page of Pinter ('You're paying for the pauses.'), thirty of *Stalingrad II – The Post-War Years*.

At last someone chose a recitation.

– Do I choose what you recite?

– No, I choose.

– So shouldn't it be cheaper than the reading?

– No. You benefit from my expertise. And get a surprise.

– Go on. I'll have a punt.

For the first time that day he could anticipate enjoyment. Free of obligation to literal clarity, mundane comprehension, he could abandon himself to his own self-pleasure.

He chose Joyce. In celebration of the spring: the Night-town chapter of *Ulysses*, segueing into the Anna Livia Plurabelle of the *Wake*, as fitting prelude to a fragrant dusk.

Warmed, attuned, he responded to vowel and syllable, the *f*s of *Liffey* feathering his lips, the *l*s of *Plurabelle* clamouring his tongue, the *v*s and *b*s vibrating his larynx, down his vertebrae, through his coccyx, the words falling moist, brine-tanged, smelling of bleach, telling a tale of scurrying waters, dappled linen, leaf, stone, rodent cry, coming to rest on a whispered *Night*.

A spat of applause brought him back, blinking in the afternoon light.

He walleted the ten pound note, counted his loose change, made his way to the kiosk for an ice cream for his throat.

As he walked to the gate he passed a knot of people grouped round a girl on her knees and a man on his back. He stopped, edged in. The girl was looking up, appealing, her hand in the man's jacket, thumb on lapel. We were chatting, she was saying, then he suddenly said Goodbye Veronica and keeled over.

Lewis felt himself a voyeur on another man's voyage, withdrew, left the park.

When he arrived home the flat was quiet. He found a note on the fridge. After a year's cohabitation he still couldn't read her writing. It appeared to read

Out of bed.

Since it was on the fridge, and the pen and Post-Its were kept on the hall table, which meant that she would have to be out of bed to write it, the note appeared to be tautological. But self-reflexive logic appealed to Lewis. As did Astra's sarcasm. (As did Astra.)

He smiled, poured himself some milk.

He had a further reading duty in the evening. There was no way of knowing when, or if, dinner would be ready. He decided to play safe, make a sandwich. The bread bin was empty. He retrieved the Post-It from the bin, reread it. Maybe it said

Out of bread.

DAVID ROSE

That would be consistent with her stock-control skills. It might also account for her absence: she had gone to the shop. He sat down to wait.

After half an hour he began to revise his interpretation. Maybe the note was an instruction. He was being instructed to go for some bread while she was busy elsewhere. It seemed more likely with each passing minute.

He took down his jacket, looked at the clock. He just had time to go to the corner shop and back, make a sandwich, rest and go out.

A wave of tiredness swept over him. Reading, as much as poetry in the old days, he found draining – something that non-artistes simply didn't understand.

He hung up his jacket, found some crackers in the cupboard, buttered them and made some tea.

He felt a little uneasy at finishing the crackers. What of Astra's meal? Then again, maybe his first reading had been correct. She may have just gone somewhere, fallen into conversation, decided on a larger-scale shopping trip. His conscience eased, he set the alarm for seven and lay down for a nap.

He got up, washed and shaved, pulled on a clean shirt, and was ready. He remembered then she was working lates.

It was a Social Capital Consolidation do, which in deference to the spring evening was done al fresco. Trestles had been laid, the street cordoned off, lights necklaced across, portable barbecues delivered.

The latter had been lit, the trestles decked, when he arrived. He reported to the party secretary, took the sealed envelope, tested the portable P.A., then sat under the strongest light bulb to open and study his lectoral assignment.

There was a reminder in the envelope that under the Conservation of Energy Initiative, their grid sector was due off at nine p.m.

Although too professional – and nervous – to eat, he accepted the proffered sausages, kebabs and vol-au-vents to take home for Astra.

As the party warmed up, he sat aside, rehearsing in his mind the opening paragraph. It was a mark of professionalism to seem not to be reading to begin with – establish audience rapport, build trust, make it appear the message was personal, meaningful, heartfelt.

He reached the point where further efforts at memorisation would be counter-productive, put the script in his pocket and tried to relax.

The secretary came across, bringing him a glass of grape juice.

– Though you might appreciate a drop of Dutch courage.

He pulled a hip flask from his jacket, pouring a liberal measure into the juice.

– Going well now. Really beginning to achieve the right *esprit de corps*, solid neighbourliness. What it's all about, wouldn't you say?

Lewis wouldn't say, partly to conserve his voice.

At eight thirty he was beckoned to the microphone. He cracked flat the script, smoothed it onto the lectern, looked up.

– We have gathered this evening as friends and neighbours with a shared commitment to neighbourly values, community spirit. We have relaxed after our day's vocation, broken bread, enjoyed the grape's yield and fellow warmth. Time now to take the wider view.

He could now allow himself to consult the script.

– The evening's theme is the means and meaning of a transparent society. It involves us all. Open government requires openness of its citizenry. We all know the problems we face. Ignorance, poverty, bad manners. For its part, the

Government is committed to their eradication. We are sometimes accused of being superficial.

He looked up, paused.

– Rightly so. We take the superficial view. We wish to bring the problems to the surface, tackle them openly, dredge up the hidden negatives, expose them to the light of progress. We aim to eliminate mystique, secrecy, prejudice, obfuscation...

Obfuscation. The word startled him. He couldn't resist repeating it, in what the audience would take to be a rhetorical flourish.

He said it slowly, tasting the syllables, the work acquiring an obscure sexual charge. He saw Astra on the bed, saw the flare of her thighs, curve of her buttocks, relived the rebuff, which no longer mattered.

He continued the reading, faltering for a moment, then feeling ahead, sentence by sentence, savouring the words.

He was enjoying this now. He began to employ *rubato*, subtle at first, then increased the changes of pace, altered the tone, acquiring gradations from irony to sarcasm with the variation of pace and volume.

The audience, barely listening at first, the speech white noise to their conversations, was now alert, following his every semantic shift.

He looked surreptitiously at his watch. Ten to nine. He was scheduled to finish at five to, allowing three minutes for a vote of thanks, then power off at nine. He doubled back, repeating paragraphs from the beginning, knowing they wouldn't have been taken in the first time, slowed down, repeated phrases in different registers, drew out the pauses.

Two minutes to nine.

The secretary was standing, behind the trestles, left arm up, cuff pulled back, his right arm describing a winding motion in the air.

Lewis read the penultimate paragraph, then announced

he was going to read it again, for maximum import.

He read it again.

Forty seconds to go as he embarked on the final, hortative paragraph. The lights dimmed momentarily, the P.A. crackled.

– What we, what society, needs, now, is a renewed commitment to civic transparency, to draw from the community's reserves of energy, its social fund of goodwill, in a bid to drag into the spotlight those lurking prejudices, shadowy resentments, to reflect and refract the Government's light of concern, ameliora...

Looking at the View

JULIET BATES

Perhaps she could call it a holiday, a short break inspired by films she had seen; journeys along highways with neon signs. But in the films the weather was yellow from the desert dust and the landscape was wide. Here, nothing was horizontal, only vertical: the broken château, the church, the white rain falling from the sky. And this town was the same as the last; the same cafe with the billiard table and stairs behind the bar, and the room with the Ricard ashtray placed on the bedside table, and the basin in the corner hidden by a screen. That was it, she thought, standing by the window. A life behind screens and veils and curtains.

There was a restaurant, but she didn't want to eat, just leave the room with the sloping ceiling. She walked to the end of the street and bought some bread in the drizzle. In a doorway she saw a boy looking out at the rain, a boy of seventeen perhaps. And as she passed he smiled a smile split by the water drops falling from the lintel above him.

The connection made things better. Lying in bed she felt something had happened in the mist, and she wondered what connections meant: brief catches of the eye, momentary smiles, flashes of recognition. She wished she were younger, or that there was more time.

In the morning she saw him again, standing on the verge

between the petrol station and the Super U. This time he held his thumb out, and she stopped because that's what they did in films, and anyway she didn't care what happened. He spoke no English and he nodded when she pointed at the road sign, and he smiled again. She studied the feeling that she had beside the boy: a feeling of familiarity, of knowing someone.

She thought, 'Is it possible that this is the son or the grandson I never had, or the lover perhaps?' and she turned to look at him. But he sat too far back, following the slick slack of the wipers, and all she saw was a breath cloud on the window opposite.

At noon she chose a service station with a café, although he didn't eat but walked around the games machines in the corner, running his hand over the screen, pressing the buttons. She bought a sandwich, something dry, ham no butter, cut it into two and ate half. She watched him, moving behind a pillar or at the window – his eel-slim shadow.

She liked their connection, her and the boy. How many years between them? Forty perhaps. She thought about complacent skin-tight youth, and the way that bodies change, how they grow angry, act against one, rebel.

In the car she considered the silence strange – for two people who knew each other well – and she started to talk. It didn't seem to matter that he couldn't understand the sounds she made. She told him her name, she told him about her holiday, her idea to keep driving south until she felt the warmth. But she knew that he didn't believe her: he stretched his leg into the well underneath the glove compartment and the gesture said, 'Tell the truth'.

She told him that she was driving south until the landscape became clearer, more horizontal, until she could see things; that it wasn't a holiday but an escape, a disappearance. She had walked out of the house, taken a train, hired a car, told no one. She said she was tired of it: tired of saying the right things, looking right, not letting the madness seep through. She told him how everything seemed like an image on paper, flat, no space, no future. She had thought the movement, the running away, might help.

The boy said nothing, he was empty faced. He moved his legs, shifting them back, hiding his feet under the gap between floor and seat. She was embarrassed too. She had made a mistake, and remembering her pleated face she took her hand from the wheel and touched it. She wanted him to go now, and she pulled off the road, saying she was tired, hoping he would get out, find another lift.

'You don't have to stay.'

But he pushed his seat back and closed his eyes, and he was so quiet she couldn't hear his breath. She watched the water slip down the windscreen in white channels, cutting the view smaller and smaller until it disappeared. She turned the mirror to see him: eyes shut, blonde hair, cream sweater. He seemed to belong to the white weather. She had imagined the connection. There was no magic link, no empathy, no closeness, and she lay back with the boy asleep beside her.

When he woke she drove on. There was no plan to her journey, no route, and it seemed that it was the same for the boy. He stared out of the window at the vertical lines: telegraph poles, fence posts, tall grass. She looked ahead at the road.

How could she get rid of him? What would happen if she stopped for the night? Would he stay in the car, come with her?

And then he said her name – 'Elizabeth' – clearly, correctly, and it surprised her. He pointed to a sign, and as if she hadn't heard, he touched her arm. She didn't want to turn off, not here, not down water-soaked, ditch-edged lanes, but the boy touched her a second time and smiled, and she pulled onto the exit ramp, into a web of roads. He lent forward, stretched out his arm, directed her with his flat hand. She was angry now: taken for granted, used, exploited. She chewed the words in her mouth and her head throbbed, 'Old woman, old woman,' like drum beats.

They seemed to circle, and the light changed and she thought, 'Maybe we are at the sea,' for she knew that the motorway skirted the coast. But his hand pushed them right: towards a dead end, a garage, shops, a railway station. A station? Why did he want a station? And she turned to say something, but he had gone, got out of the car, left the door swinging on its hinges. He'd gone without smiling goodbye and she wasn't sorry.

She sat for a while looking through the windscreen, noticing that the rain had stopped. She thought about going home, turning round, catching a train, reeling in the line she had made. She got out, crossed the road and now she heard two languages – one more foreign than the other. She watched the departures board shuffle words and names she did not know. Here it smelled different. Not like the other places. Dryer, sharper, more acid. She couldn't see the boy.

She walked back to the car, breathing deeply, trying to clear her head, looking at the view: a parked lorry, a road that changed to a tarmac path, a footbridge, a thick band of hills. She walked onto the footbridge.

'This is the border,' she thought. 'If I go to the other side I shall be somewhere else,' and she walked into the middle and saw the hills cleave. They slipped down to a valley leaving a 'v' of space.

Contributors

Charlotte Allan has mostly written plays, for stage and occasionally radio, including *Only Available in Carlisle* produced by Theatre by the Lake, Keswick. She currently lives in Glasgow where she works in youth theatre, walks in parks and plays the cello very poorly.

Juliet Bates lives in Paris and teaches at the Ecole des Beaux-Arts in Caen, Normandy. Her short stories have been published in a number of literary magazines in Britain and Canada.

Annie Clarkson is a poet, social worker and short story writer living in Manchester. Her collection of prose poems *Winter Hands* was published by Shadowtrain Books in 2007.

Adam Connors won second prize in the London Writer's Competition (2005), and was longlisted for the Fish Short Story Prize (2006). His stories have appeared in a number of journals and anthologies, and his articles in *Flavorpill, ItchyLondon,* and *Null Hypothesis.* He was technical advisor to the stage show, *Stephen Hawking's Brief History of Time*, and taught Science and Agriculture in Sudan for a while.

Steve Dearden's short stories have appeared in anthologies and magazines in the UK, Australia and Finland. He was one of six writers from the UK and Finland who collaborated on *Interland*, published by Smith Doorstop. He coordinates international exchanges and is a director of the Writing Squad.

Paul de Havilland lives in Edinburgh. 'Carousel' is his third published short story. He teaches business skills.

Tyler Keevil was raised in Vancouver, Canada. He first came to the UK in 1999 to study English at Lancaster University. Since then, his short fiction has appeared in a variety of magazines, including *Cambrensis*, *Transmission*, and *New Welsh Review*. He currently lives in Wales, where he is undertaking his MA in Creative Writing at Aberystwyth University.

Chris Killen was born in 1981. He is currently living in Manchester. His first novel, *The Bird Room*, will be published by Canongate, in spring 2009. He also writes a blog: www.dayofmoustaches.blogspot.com

Richard Knight was born and brought up on the east coast but moved to Saddleworth 17 years ago where he still lives with his wife, two children and one dog. He writes both adult and children's fiction. One of his adult stories was included in *Arc Short Stories vol. 9* (Ed. Sarah Dunant and Tibor Fischer) in 1998 and his first children's book is to be published by Barefoot Books in 2008.

Jacqueline McCarrick's first play, *The Mushroom Pickers*, premiered at the Southwark Playhouse in London in May 2006. Her second play, *The Moth-Hour*, was short-listed for the 2006 Sphinx Playwriting Award, and was presented at the Irish Repertory Theatre in New York in January 2007. Her poetry and short stories have been published in various magazines and anthologies.

Neil McQuillian is from Liverpool, but is living in London for the time being. His story is dedicated to his Uncle Richie.

Heather Richardson is one of three featured writers in *Short Story Introductions 1* (Lagan Press, 2007). She is a former winner of the Brian Moore Short Story Award, and has been shortlisted for a number of other prizes, including Asham, Fish and the Kaos Films Short Screenplay prizes. She was also runner up in the Cardiff International Poetry Competition (2007). She lives in Belfast.

David Rose lives in London, and has had fiction published in the *Literary Review, Panurge, Main Street Journal, Odyssey, Front and Centre, Zembla, Neon Lit: the Time Out Book of New Writing, You Are Here* (ed. Bill Broady & Jane Metcalfe), and the Canadian anthology *Grunt and Groan*.

Guy Russell was born in Chatham, lives in Milton Keynes, and works at the Open University. He has had stories in *Prop* and *Northern Stories*, and reviews poetry for *Tears in the Fence*. His fifteenth unpublished novel is about student animal rights activists.

Guy Ware is a recovering civil servant. He has published stories in prize collections and other anthologies and is a regular contributor to the 'Tales of the Decongested' story readings at Foyles book shop in London. In April, he will feature as one of *Six New Voices* in a new collection from Apis Books.

Acknowledgements

This book would not have been possible without the support and advice of the following people: Sarah Eyre, Isaac Shaffer, David Eckersall, Alba Griffin, Colin Jones, Carole Buchan, Bill Broady, Will Carr, Avril Heffernan, Helen McGenity, and Dorothy Taylor at Business in the Arts North West.

Special thanks are owed to Gillian Knox for her patience and understanding.

Parenthesis
a new generation in fiction
Edited by Ra Page

ISBN 0 9548280 7 0
RRP: £7.95

Rampaging behemoths, giant, washed-up fishtails, mysterious briefcases, role-playing cuddly toys... The world of the short story is a weird and wonderful one, made even stranger by the unique assortment of characters that crop up in them. Incongruity seems to be their secret ingredient - or rather the right kind of incongruity, an artful one that punctuates the flat realism of most literature and inserts an isolated moment, an atomised truth.

The second in Comma's bi-annual showcase of new writers brings together 20 of the most imaginative and daring voices taking up the form; writers dedicated to charting the far reaches of this terrain right at the outset of their careers; writers who prove it's best to stay short.

"Reasserts and cherishes the short story form's ingrained oddness, its unique kind of drama and its potential to surprise."
- *Independent on Sunday*

"Takes readers on nail-biting adventures... vital and imaginative."
- *Big Issue*

"This book is a true rarity."
- *Aethetica Magazine*

The Independent Consultant's Survival Guide

Starting up and succeeding as a self-employed consultant

Mike Johnson

Mike Johnson is the managing partner of Johnson & Associates, a corporate communications firm that he founded in 1982 in Brussels and London, following a career in journalism and corporate communication for multinational corporations. His work today centres around talent management, organizational development and corporate communication for private and public organizations. He is the author of nine books on business and management issues, and has developed a series of World of Work studies for the *Financial Times* and *The Economist*. His most recent books are *Winning the People Wars* (2001), *Talent Magnet* (2002) and *The New Rules of Engagement* (2004). A regular at conferences and seminars around the globe, at which he lectures on emerging world of work issues and trends, he is the founder of the Independent, Global think-tank and The FutureWork Forum.

Dedication

To Neil, Nick and Rai, for their encouragement, assistance and friendship.

The Chartered Institute of Personnel and Development is the leading publisher of books and reports for personnel and training professionals, students, and all those concerned with the effective management and development of people at work. For details of all our titles, please contact the publishing department:

Tel: 020 8612 6204

E-mail: publish@cipd.co.uk

The catalogue of all CIPD titles can be viewed on the CIPD website:

www.cipd.co.uk/bookstore